THE EVIL THAT BOYS DO

THE
EVIL
THAT
BOYS
DO

T.C. Van Adler

alyson books
los angeles

MANUFACTURED IN THE UNITED STATES OF AMERICA.

THIS TRADE PAPERBACK ORIGINAL IS PUBLISHED BY ALYSON PUBLICATIONS,
P.O. BOX 4371, LOS ANGELES, CALIFORNIA 90078-4371.
DISTRIBUTION IN THE UNITED KINGDOM BY TURNAROUND PUBLISHER SERVICES LTD.,
UNIT 3, OLYMPIA TRADING ESTATE, COBURG ROAD, WOOD GREEN,
LONDON N22 6TZ ENGLAND.

FIRST EDITION: MAY 2003

03 04 05 06 07 **a** 10 9 8 7 6 5 4 3 2 1

ISBN 1-55583-660-7

LIBRARY OF CONGRESS CATALOGING-IN-PUBLICATION DATA

VAN ADLER, T. C.
THE EVIL THAT BOYS DO / T.C. VAN ADLER.—1ST ED.
ISBN 1-55583-660-7
1. CORRECTIONS—CONTRACTING OUT—FICTION. 2. ART HISTORIANS—FICTION.
3. TRANSSEXUALS—FICTION. 4. PENNSYLVANIA—FICTION. 5. PRISONERS—FICTION.
6. PRISONS—FICTION. 7. CLERGY—FICTION. I. TITLE.
PS 3572.A4136E94 2003
813'.54—DC21   2002043777

CREDITS

COVER IMAGE FROM CARAVAGGIO'S *THE HOLY FAMILY*.
COVER DESIGN BY MATT SAMS.

Cast of Characters

Others

Bryn Mawr College
Dr. Charles Mitchum, Art Historian

Parish
Monsignor Duhmbelle

Spiritual Director
Father Avertanus Deblaer, Emeritus Professor of Mystical Theology

One

IN PRISON, THE CRUDEST OBJECTS SOMETIMES become precious beyond belief. Take, for example, the little steel-framed mirror that hung in Father Brocard's office. When he took over the position of Catholic chaplain at Brotherly Love Penitentiary, just after the untimely and suspicious death of his predecessor, the mirror was simply part of the unfortunate clutter in his sad little cinder-block room. Not that Brocard had been used to luxurious digs. The cell that had all but collapsed around him in the Monastery of San Redempto in Rome, where he had spent more years of his life than most inmates have sentences, had been on the bleak side as well. But at least it had had a window that afforded a glimpse of the outside world. Brotherly Love Pen, modern as it was, promised no such luxuries. Granted, a large window of bulletproof glass had been built into one wall of his office. That grim orifice looked out onto the narrow corridor leading into the chapel so that the guards might occasionally check in on the light-deprived chaplain. It was a sadistic design touch that offered neither privacy nor security. In no way could it be considered a real window. However, Father Brocard did have that mirror.

How the mirror got there no one knew. Glass was forbidden behind bars. Inmates who chose to have them were given ersatz mirrors, polished bits of metal that gave carnival reflections in exchange for a gaze. For some reason, the officers of Custody, who were on Brocard's case about every other little matter, were unconcerned about the mirror. Their unconcern persisted even as inmates began to gravitate to it. Even on slow days, Father Brocard counted on inmates to pop into his office on their way to the gym or to the hospital for a brief hello and a long look at themselves in the mirror. "Looking tight"—prison-speak for "good"—was always the verdict because, curiously, the general population of Brotherly Love Pen was uncommonly self-involved and inordinately fond of itself. The men were incapable of seeing anything clearly, even their own reflections.

Being a rather formal fellow, Brocard referred to his precious mirror as "the chaplain's looking glass." The allusion to Lewis Carroll's Alice was deliberate. It had not taken him long to realize that going to prison was for him every bit as life-altering as a trip to the world behind the looking glass, where nothing was as it seemed to be.

How he came to be at Brotherly Love still puzzled him. And why he felt so very at home in that decidedly perverse place was an even greater mystery. He had moved back to the States after his years in Rome not only because the monastery where he lived had literally collapsed—reason enough for a change of scenery, to be sure. His move was also a consequence of his involvement in the retrieval and authentication of the great Poussin painting of Saint Agatha that now hung in the Louvre. That case and its toll on the emotions would have taken a great deal out of anyone—not least a monk. And, despite the unfortunate demise of his monastery and his enforced separation from the few remaining members of his community, Brocard still considered himself to be just that: a monk.

Shortly after he took the position as prison chaplain, Brocard sent an E-mail to his old friend Father Avertanus Deblaer, once a distinguished professor of mystical theology, now retired to the order's nursing home in Nijmegen, in the far east of Holland. Dotty and antiquated as Avertanus might seem, he had flung himself into cyberspace to escape into the real world. In truth, his eccentricity disguised a mind as clever as it was keen.

Caro Avertanus,

By time you read this I will be in jail. Don't worry for me though, my old friend—it is a self-imposed sentence. And one which, I must admit, secretly excites me. As you know, I have been going rather batty at Our Lady of Perpetual Help. Not that Bryn Mawr isn't restful beyond belief. It is order itself, and you know how compulsive I can be. Nor even that the pastor, the ever-distant Monsignor Duhmbelle, is getting on my nerves. He says Mass, signs a few checks, and does a quick nine holes before vanishing for the day completely. Nothing too taxing there, for him or me. No, if truth be known, I miss the excitement of the hunt: our strange art-historian friend Zinka and her boundless energy, the unsolved problems and the obstacles thrown up at every turn, and the unadulterated evil of the worlds of money and art. In a word, caro Avertanus, I was nearly becoming bored.

Then, *mirabile dictu,* I received a call from a priest at the chancery, which for some unknown reason has changed its name to pastoral center. Don't ask and don't get me started. Anyway, this Father Something-or-Other was trolling around looking for a priest (any priest obviously, as I was surely at the very end of the diocesan list) to say Mass in a prison. Not just any prison it seems. This one happened to be the high-profile private prison opened just a few years ago in the heart of Pennsylvania Dutch country. My sister tells me there was quite a flap about it at the time. But the company that owns the facility calmed the preservationists by designing the exterior buildings to look like large barns, hiding much of the razor wire behind hedges, and dotting the fields around it with sheep and cows. More perversely still, they gave it the name of Brotherly Love Correctional Facility.

Anyway, off I went to jail the week before last. Initially, there was no more to it than checking in for an international flight—the metal detector, questions, and cursory check of documents and tote bag. But when the first and then second gates of metal opened and closed behind me, a chill went through me and I knew for certain that, mercifully, I wasn't in Bryn Mawr anymore. What impressed me when I was escorted into the chapel area was how well organized it was. I had brought my portable Mass kit with me, but it was not needed. The first chaplain, who had served until his untimely death a couple of months ago, had purchased everything that was needed. Not of the quality we were used to at San Redempto, to be sure, but fully serviceable objects. It seems the plan at Brotherly Love Pen is to offer the young men—our average age is 25, by the way—opportunities to better themselves educationally and spiritually. Not just, as the corrections people have it, to warehouse them. That excited me enormously. So, too, did the opportunity to build a community of faith for a collection of convicted felons. Staffing my office with rapists and murderers also brings a certain thrill.

Every day, my old friend, is a new adventure in here. In truth, I don't yet have any idea what is expected of me and whether I will be effective in this ministry. But what a strange new world it is. Happily, they have allowed me a computer so that I can write the many reports that have to be presented weekly, prepare authorized absences for inmates who wish to see me (although between us they seem to get around just fine without any authorization), and to receive daily E-mails from the CEO of Prison World, Inc., the private company that owns and operates Brotherly Love Pen. I cannot leave the computer unattended, as my clerk, when I hire him, will have access to it. But Rome was good training for me. I know how to keep my eyes open. The good news is that you can now contact me here directly and, should some new crime-solving project come our way—and how could it not in such an auspicious place?—I will be able to contact you immediately.

That is all for now, dear Avertanus. I hope the rattles of death around you don't keep you up at night and that your research, in whatever direction it is now going, proceeds smoothly. My love to any of our friends you might meet in cyberspace.

Father Brocard did not realize how prophetic his words were. Nor could he know that the harrowing adventure that awaited him at this prison in the farmlands of Pennsylvania would present even greater challenges than the recovery of Poussin's *St. Agatha's Breast.*

Two

HE TRIED HARD TO ACT AS IF HE WERE IN CONTROL. But the truth was, he simply wasn't. What's more, they knew it.

It had started off harmlessly enough. Shortly after he had opened his office for the day—after gliding through the metal detector in the lobby, through three sets of gates and a host of guards—an inmate asked to use the chapel for prayer. The fact that he had not seen this inmate at services, Bible study, or any of the programs offered by chaplaincy didn't concern Brocard greatly. There were nearly a thousand inmates at Brotherly Love Pen, all dressed in gray. And Brocard was the first to confess he had difficulty with names and faces at best of times.

The chapel was a cavernous hole of a place, old beyond its years. Its pews were already scarred with graffiti, and their kneelers were falling off (the hardware made excellent weapons or *shanks*). Half the feeble ceiling lights were burnt out. After numerous calls to the maintenance department, it became clear to Brocard that nothing would happen until total darkness prevailed. The chapel's only decoration was the cross hanging ponderously over the stage area that served as a sanctuary. The cross's most distinctive feature was a pop-off corpus that enabled Protestants and Catholics alike to worship without insult. Also in the chapel were a portable altar (which Brocard came to refer to as Meals-On-Wheels) and a mobile baptismal pool which everyone referred to as the Jacuzzi since, well, it was often used in that way.

No sooner had he returned to his office to turn on his computer than a second, a third, then four or five more inmates sneaked past his office into the chapel. Brocard had been told that, except for major services, inmates were supposed to be on a list authorizing them to be off their cell tiers. But here were at least a dozen, linking hands in the sanctuary and chanting something that, reassuringly, seemed to be about Jesus.

Loosen up, Brocard, he cautioned himself. *Life is not as orderly as you would like it to be. What is wrong with a little hollering to God occasionally? A little spontaneous expression of faith?* Still, he had his suspicions as he moved closer to inspect the group.

The praying inmates had compressed themselves into a huddle—more of a scrum really—so tightly configured that no one else could enter. Ever curious, Brocard climbed up on the front pew to see what, if anything, was happening in there. He was, after all, responsible for his space—that was part of his job description—and someone might just ask him what on earth was going on. There was something inside. From what he could see, neck craned and body raised as high as he could manage, there was a small inmate kneeling with hands upraised in the center of the group. Tears streamed down his face. Was this poor fellow being trampled to death? Or, ludicrously, was he the object of their worship? There was simply no way of telling.

At first Brocard thought the assembled group was composed entirely of black inmates. Only when he drew close to them and listened to their prayers did he realize they were dark-complexioned Dominicanos and Cubanos. These inmates were fiercely Hispanic, as were the prayers they offered. There were enough similarities between Italian—Brocard's language of choice—and Spanish to give him some idea of just how disturbing their incantations were.

In spontaneous, overlapping exclamations, first one inmate then another cried out for San Ramón Nonato to be with him, or Santa Clara or Santa Teresita. Several chanted together, *"Ruega por nosotros"*—"Pray for us." Others called upon the help of the Virgen de la Candelaria. In itself this was nothing. A litany of sorts, chaotic to be sure, but not unlike the frequent litanies that peppered services at San Redempto. It was when they started to *command* the saints—there is no other word for it—to bring down their curse on the institution, to wage battle with the demon prowling in their midst, that Brocard became concerned. Wasn't there something in the officers' handbook—the spine of which he hadn't cracked—about conspiracy to incite a riot?

Of course, Brocard knew himself well enough to think he might be overreacting. Still, as the words *"trae tu maldición"*—"bring down your curse"—rang out (and as the little figure crushed in the midst of the pious scrum cried out, *"El Demonio! El Demonio!"*), he felt he had to act. But what exactly was he to do?

Fortunately, just as he was about to take some perilous and inappropriate action, he caught sight of Andy, his clerk, at the chapel door. In the dispassionate and cocky way of all inmates, Andy signaled him to retreat to the office, where he filled in Brocard on what was happening.

"It's only Jesucito and his apostles," Andy said in the most exasperatingly casual way.

"And who exactly might this Baby Jesus be?" Brocard asked, trying his best as he took his seat behind his desk to appear equally unconcerned.

"Not sure really. The priest before you, Father Norm, couldn't really get to the bottom of it. They descend on the chapel occasionally, usually just before some disaster strikes. They scream a lot and then flop around like fish."

"When might I expect that?"

"Oh, you won't have to wait long. They're in and out within 10 or 15. No use stopping them. A pretty nasty bunch. But harmless enough in their own way." Then, reaching under the desk for his heating coil, Andy prepared to boil some water for his Earl Grey. Contraband, of course, but for Andy such things were no problem. "Tea?"

"Not a bad idea." Brocard was eager to put this episode behind him. But, as the incantations reached fever pitch, he knew that more than a cup of tea was in order.

At least Andy had helped him get a handle on what was happening. This wasn't the first time—and far from the last—Andy had translated the arcane language of prison-speak to spare Brocard from painfully embarrassing mistakes. Curious person, Andy: Irish to the bone, a well-spoken boy. Almost human. Except that he'd had a prosperous business that had been corrupt to the core by all accounts. And he was a cold-blooded murderer who waxed almost rhapsodic about the carnage he had wrought.

"Fascinating to see brains splattered on a wall," he had told Brocard in one of their first talks. "Particles everywhere, highlighted with specks of red. And one piece of shattered skull lodged into the wall, white on white outdoing anything Pollock could have imagined. I almost did the kid a favor. He was never so beautiful in life."

Andy *did* have his good points. He had been the late Father Norm's clerk and knew the many ins and outs of the job. And, as he was quick to point out, he was one of the few inmates with a brain—or at least with a formal education. Before his fall from grace, Andy had moved in only the best academic and social circles. And since his incarceration, he had jailed well, learning the vocabulary and the behaviors necessary to survive and even prosper. For Brocard, this meant that Andy, despite his admittedly cynical ways, was invaluable in speaking both languages: those of the street and the joint.

As suddenly as it had all begun, the chapel fell silent and the inmates disbanded. One by one they passed the office window, each in his own way avoiding eye contact with Brocard. Not being one who needed the spark of human contact—a couple of decades in a monastery could knock the pep out of anyone—he was not offended. It did, however, increase his suspicion that they were up to no good, despite Andy's disclaimer. As they left, he opened his file drawer, took out his "pending" folder, and pretended to be at work.

"Excuse me, Father Brocard?" The sound of a woman's voice—and an educated one at that—came as a surprise. Somehow in the midst of the gray shirts, a slender, attractive woman, professional in dress and bearing, had appeared at his door. "Allow me to introduce myself. Dr. Kris Pouri, head of Psychology."

"Please come in," he said, rising without pausing for breath. "Tea?"

How awkward the whole thing was. Had he forgotten all his social skills in a few short weeks? Here was an attractive woman, smiling awkwardly at the door, not even sure she had the right man. She was not yet even in the room, not even seated, and he offered her a tea.

"A man who wastes no time," she said puckishly, taking the seat across from him. "Tea would be lovely, thank you."

"I'll send the porter to the kitchen for milk and sugar," Andy said commandingly. Then, picking up the stinger and cups, he assured Brocard he would be back with the tea presently as he closed the door behind them.

"Interesting they allow you to have a mirror. And rather macabre, if you don't mind my saying, that you still have a picture of the dead priest on your wall." Then, looking slightly embarrassed, she added, "Sorry. You didn't know the poor man, did you?"

"No, not at all," Brocard reassured her. "Did you know him?"

"Only slightly. He was a distant creature. Kept very much to himself. He once told me there were some things he wanted to talk over. Private things. I cringed to think what they might be. Then," she perked up a bit as she finished her tale, "he was dead."

"Just like that?"

"Poof! Out like a light. There was some talk, you know, but Prison World is not too big on negative press, in case you didn't know. So heart attack, I think they said, and voilà—the case was closed."

Such a lighthearted, attractive soul, Brocard thought as he watched her. *A little sinister to be sure, but what's not to like about that?*

Turning to see that the door was shut, she caught sight of Jesucito—the little Hispanic who had nearly been crushed in prayer—making his way out of the chapel. He had the most self-effacing way about him, like a novice whose identity has been stripped away. Downcast gaze and shoulders bent toward the ground in semblance of perfect humility.

"Keep your eye on him, Father. We suspect he's self-mutilating. He's more likely to be found in your domain than mine until he cracks."

"It will be hard for me to avoid him. Jesucito, I think they call him."

"Among 30 or so aliases. Quite a jacket."

"Jacket?" Brocard was still new to the metalanguage of his new job.

"File: his whole record from JOC—Judgment of Conviction—to current progress notes." There was no edge in her tone. Nothing to prove. A refreshing change from so many others he had met in the prison.

"His last offense is rather amusing on paper, if not for the victim." As Brocard signaled Andy to come into the office with the tea, some packets of sugar, and a carton of milk, Doctor Pouri bit her lip, waiting for privacy.

"Hard to imagine him—Jesucito, that is—being violent at all," Brocard volunteered as Andy closed the door behind him. At this a broad smile crossed her face.

"He has a string of major felonies, none of which indicates he is mild-mannered. The one that landed him here was when he accosted an Amish girl in Blue Balls."

"Unfortunate name."

"Isn't it just? As ironic as hers." Reading the question in his eyes, she said, "Chastity."

"Couldn't be."

"Would I lie to a priest? Anyway, he tried to rob Chastity in Blue Balls, and as she had no pockets or zippers—"

"Very Pennsylvania Dutch."

"Isn't it, though? You probably guessed it, she said she had no money on her, and he didn't believe her, and he began groping around trying to find some money and, wouldn't you know it, an off-duty cop passed by, and he got booked for intent to do sexual assault."

"All that and no money."

"Life is so unfair." Then, taking a sip of her tea, she moved her chair closer to the desk and in lowered voice, as contrived as it was dramatic, said, "But that is not why I came to see you. It's about another inmate, no more disturbed perhaps, but of far greater immediate concern." She paused a moment to collect her thoughts.

"Are you familiar with the Ad Seg Unit?" Seeing Brocard at a loss, she explained. "There are nearly 50 inmates here who for one reason or another are kept apart from the general population. For their own good, although they themselves often see it as a punishment."

Brocard began to explain how he had not yet gotten around to exploring all of the areas of the jail because it was so hard for him to get away from the chapel area. But Doctor Pouri did not let him finish. Her information was more urgent than his excuses.

"Recently, Tony Polluto, a common pederast, was placed in Ad Seg because the *ñetas,* one of the Hispanic gangs, found out he had molested a young boy."

"So they had to hurt him?"

"Exactly." Doctor Pouri was relieved Father Brocard knew something about the new world he inhabited. "They have a code of so-called honor that tells them to slash up anyone who has harmed a woman or child."

"Which is probably most of them as well?"

"Right again. But this goes back to fussing about the speck in someone else's eye without taking note of the plank in your own—which I believe lies in your domain."

Smiling in agreement, Brocard sipped his own tea, which had finally cooled enough for him to drink. Doctor Pouri continued.

"Some of the officers reported Tony was having delusions that angels were descending on him to torment him for having desecrated the Nativity."

"That's a new one. How exactly might that be done?"

"My question exactly. So, armed with my trusty *DSM,* the psychologists' Bible, I went off to see him."

"Is it usual for you to visit an inmate's cell?"

"Highly unusual. But given the threats around him and the fact that an officer stood guard the whole time, custody also thought it best they not move him."

"Doctor Pouri," Brocard ventured after a brief pause, "I am flattered that you have come to visit—flattered beyond words that you have taken me into your confidence. But," here he paused again, not wanted to offend his new, clever, and attractive friend. "I don't see how I can help you with a delusional inmate. I am not trained in psychology at all." Then he wished he had kept his mouth shut and allowed her to think him clever as well.

"Caravaggio." Her pronunciation was impeccable, her tone rang clear.

"Pardon."

"Caravaggio. Tony Polluto is convinced he has something to do with the disappearance or destruction of a Caravaggio Nativity."

"And what does this have to do with me?" Brocard asked, his puzzlement growing by the moment.

"Come now, Father Brocard," Doctor Pouri said, with a coyness that belied her professional demeanor. "I know about you."

"You know what?" he said. For a moment he'd forgotten who he was.

"The *New York Observer* article?" Seeing this made no impression, she pushed on. "*St. Agatha?*" At this his face lit up.

"You read about it?"

"Granted many of the yokels out here haven't a clue, but really, Father Brocard, who do you think I am?"

"Actually, I just met you—" he started to say. But she wouldn't hear of it.

"No, no you cannot hide from me. So exciting. Art. Murder. Theft. Authentication. Vindication."

"Well, yes." He was wistful now, "it was quite wonderful."

"That's why I thought of you right away. Tony was quite insistent about some sort of a conspiracy, and that this Caravaggio painting could bring down God's wrath on him and others if it is not returned."

"But you said he was delusional."

"Crazier things have happened. Anyway, he sounded so convincing to me, and he didn't display any other paranoid behavior. I think it would be worth our while…" She hesitated, then reconsidered, "Worth *your* while to pay him a visit."

"If you think I should, of course I will."

"Good. Here is his number and cell. Ad Seg is just past Center Control, second gate on the left." Then, as she stood to leave, she added rather ominously, "See him soon. I hear he is increasingly depressed. You know how strange this place makes people. Anything might happen."

Andy opened the door. Both Doctor Pouri and Brocard wondered whether he had eavesdropped on their conversation. Too late now, even if he had. This was a prison, after all.

"Well, Father, it looks like you are becoming an important person."

"What do you mean?" Brocard was still preoccupied with what the beautiful doctor had told him. "Just a visit from a colleague."

"The head of Psychology coming to you. Is that the mountain coming to Muhammad or what? Big person in here, Doctor Pouri. Wields a lot of power."

"Seems a good and fair person as well," Brocard added.

"I wouldn't know anything about either of those two things." Even when he joked there was something creepy about Andy. "Still, you're the man."

"You mean," Brocard said looking up at the photograph above his desk, "Father Norm has been forgotten?"

At that Andy leapt up and in an almost balletic move lifted the picture off its hook and placed it in the top drawer of his desk. "Dead and buried." Then, with a smile as broad as it was insincere, he added, "You boss priest, you're the man."

"Yes," Brocard repeated in a hollow voice. "Yes, ready or not, I guess I am."

Three

"SO PRETTY. NOW, TELL ME THAT ISN'T PRETTY."

Brocard did wish inmates were better mannered. They just popped into his office at the least convenient time and "got in your face," as they were wont to say. More exasperating still, they often took no notice of him at all, preferring to admire themselves in the looking glass. It was enough to make any chaplain long for the good old days of maximum security lockdown for all, when missions of mercy to cells were the norm.

"So, Dean," he said, valiantly attempting to bring the inmate out of himself while maintaining a casual, almost disinterested composure. "Why is it you are called 'the Nose' when, for all I can see, your nose is neither large nor distinguished."

"It's not the way it looks." It was clear Dean was as happy to talk about himself, as he was to look at himself. "It's the way I can use it." In one fluid gesture, he reversed and straddled the plastic chair by the door and pointed to his nose for dramatic emphasis. "How I use it."

"Nothing more than to smell with, I hope." Although he was schooled in natural law—in which everything has its inviolable, God-given purpose—Brocard had become resigned to the fact that natural law rarely found its way into Brotherly Love Pen.

"Oh yeah, all those things as well," Dean said rather cockily, leaving Brocard totally perplexed. "No, the nose thing comes out of my crime. Or what I'm in for."

"Which is?" By now it had become clear that to Brocard his plans to rush over to see Tony the Tree Jumper were coming undone. *My God,* he thought, *now I'm doing it, too.* He had acquired the habit of sticking labels on everyone, like objects in some perverse discount store. Still, he was in Ad Seg and going nowhere. As was Andy the clerk, who was happily taking in Brocard's private conversation with Dean, while defragging the computer in an attempt to look busy. Brocard coughed to get his attention, but Dean, an exhibitionist of epic proportions, brushed off his concern. These were men, after all, whose shared space is dominated by a toilet. Enough said.

"I had my suspicions, you see, that the mother of my kids was getting herself knocked up by someone. Just couldn't figure out who. So when she went out one day, I followed her. You know, I just knew she was up to something. So I trailed her."

A run-of-the-mill stalker, Brocard thought. Even had that intense, crazed look about him that marks a man obsessed. And the long pauses, that was telling too. It was almost as if Dean were thrilling to the memory, playing the tape in his mind, and pumping blood into the divots at his temples until it shone pinkly beneath his colorless skin. *Maybe,* Brocard thought, *this was not just your normal stalker.*

"So the bitch," Dean began, before catching himself— interesting what a Roman collar can still do—and smiling wryly before going on. "Excuse me, Father. So the trashy young lady goes into this project—you know, the one in North Philly—and I wait for a few minutes and go in after her." Brocard leaned forward. The story was becoming interesting and the reason for the nickname "Nose" was finally becoming clear.

"So I take the elevator up to the top floor and then go from door to door," Dean continued.

"You were knocking at every apartment?" Brocard was appalled by Dean's audacity. For a monk, privacy was paramount.

"No. Smelling."

"What exactly do you mean, smelling?"

"Like a dog. I got down on my knees and stuck my nose under each door until I smelt her out."

Even though he had heard the story countless times before, it was clear Andy was enjoying it immensely. As for Father Brocard, he could hardly wait to E-mail his friend Avertanus about this one.

"And you located her this way?"

"You bet your—" Dean began before catching himself again. "Yup. Sure did."

"I hope you don't mind my asking," Brocard replied cautiously, "but did your young lady have—how can I put it—an unusual scent? An acrid air about her?"

"Everyone does. You just have to have the nose." It was evident Dean was proud of his gifted nose. "And when her wimpy friend opened the door, I caught her there, even though she said they were old school friends and even though they had all their clothes on. Well, anyway, I knew, so I had to punish her for it, you know. And mess him up bad, too."

Brocard found the thought of this lanky creature working his nose around floor after floor of door frames in a housing project perverse enough. The fact that he actually located and then pulverized two people who were presumably just chatting about old times was beyond all comprehension.

"And you don't feel—excuse me if I sound Catholic here, but I *am* a priest—you don't feel any guilt about things? About hurting these two people?"

"I wasn't the one screwing around, Father." Dean was obviously perplexed by the question. "But," he said, clearly wanting to change the subject, "that was not why I stopped by." Barely pausing for breath, he forged on. "What can you tell me about the red heifer?"

Without a moment's consideration, Brocard, a man without guile, said, "Nothing."

Dean saw Brocard's reply as a sign of ignorance at best, indifference at worse.

"The red heifer," he repeated slowly, as if drawing out the words for a slow child. "Numbers 19." At this, Andy took a Bible off the shelf and handed it to Dean, who had been born again in prison and was particularly adept at locating a raft of verses. "You don't have the real Bible? The King James?"

"Sorry," Brocard offered, although not very sincerely. "Take my word for it: The New American is a fine translation. Very scholarly." Dean mumbled something to himself, clearly upset at not being able to read the Word as God Himself had written it.

"I'll come back later with a real Bible. You have to know about this. Officer Thomas has this really interesting interpretation of what it all means."

Then, with a quick look into the mirror on his way out, Dean was gone.

"More doom and gloom. Still," Brocard said as he gathered his things for a trip to Ad Seg, "Dean the Nose is harmless enough."

"But just watch your back, Father," Andy said, a strange, ominous note in his voice. "He'll get you whatever way he can."

four

IT WAS A RELIEF TO LEAVE THE OFFICE AND VENTURE into the prison. Freedom would hardly be the word for it although, in truth, Brocard felt his freedom more keenly in that place than he ever could "on the street," where liberty was so heedlessly spent and so lightly esteemed.

A short distance from the chapel was Central Control, the command unit through which everyone in the prison—staff, custody, and inmates—was monitored. The degree of control exerted by Central Control was tenuous because of the seemingly enlightened, almost laissez-faire policy laid down by the Warden, Tamara Boggs. She was a well-meaning woman who had acquired exactly the wrong amount of education: not enough to develop an inquisitive mind, but just enough to make her believe she had all the answers. So despite the best intentions of the lieutenant and his cohorts in Center Control, inmates came and went more or less at will, gates between the units sprang open at the least pressure, and, in this unwisely libertine environment, chaos was beginning to reign.

To Brocard's benign, naive mind, all this appeared to be nothing more than the healthy bustle of activity. Inmates passed him with food carts as he made his way past the movement control officer. A small group of Hispanic inmates paused in their plotting to wave to him as he made his way down the long corridor past the mess hall. *Not so different from the refectory at San Redempto,* he thought. *Could do with a large crucifix—and without the guards in riot gear in the observation cage—but otherwise, really quite similar.*

The gate to the Administrative Segregation Unit was wide open, so Brocard walked right in and presented himself at the officer's desk. It was Thomas: Just his luck.

"Yes, sir," Thomas growled. "What is it you want?"

Thomas was one of those do-it-yourself Christians. He had never able to find a church that was right for him—which meant, of course, that the churches were all wrong. He had told Father Brocard shortly after meeting him that Matthew 23 prohibited him from calling anyone "Father" except the Father in heaven. When Brocard asked him why Jesus himself, who often spoke in language meant to teach by deliberately shocking listeners, called Abraham "Father," Thomas realized whom he was talking to. "Get behind me, Satan," were among his first words to Brocard. And the relationship between the two men never progressed any further. If nothing else, Officer Thomas was steadfast in his belief.

"I have been asked to check in on an inmate." Brocard took out the slip of paper Doctor Pouri had given him so as to be as official as possible. "The inmate's name is T. Polluto."

"He's sound asleep," Thomas replied, stone-faced.

Not willing to be thwarted, yet not wanting to be too officious, Father Brocard asked whether Polluto had been asleep for long.

"A couple of days, from what I can see. Sleeps straight through count." Several times a day, all inmates returned to their cells to be counted by the guards. Heaven forbid any of these souls escape into the fertile farmlands of Intercourse, Pennsylvania. No telling what mischief they might get up to.

"Seems a bit unusual to me, Officer. Meds or not. Wake him up for me."

By the inflection in his voice, Brocard made it clear this was a command, not a request. Officer Thomas had a way of pressing all Brocard's buttons. And he had read the Prison World Code and knew his rights.

Seething at the thought of taking commands from the prince of darkness himself—in the guise of an Irishman, at that—Officer Thomas took his keys off his belt and led Brocard to Room 13. As they passed the small Plexiglas windows in the cell doors on each side, Brocard made something resembling a papal blessing to the inmates who called out to him. (He was awkwardly uncertain about what exactly he was to do). Although their voices were muffled by the steel doors and speaking grates, their cries were sharper and infinitely more plaintive than any he'd heard in his office.

As they approached Tony's door, the fluorescent tube in the center of the hallway blew out, emitting a loud, frightening pop, not unlike the sound of a gunshot on a still night. In the pool of darkness, Officer Thomas had difficulty finding the right key and opening the door. But not as much difficulty as he had getting Tony to wake up. After several loud, bellowed commands, one nudge, and a firm kick, Father Brocard took over.

He shoved aside the officer and bent down to feel for a pulse.

"He is dead, Officer. Stone-dead, and has been for quite some time."

"You are the devil incarnate."

"Please, don't be silly at a time like this. Just call Center Control and get them to do what they have to do." As he turned to leave, Brocard pulled out the oils he always kept with him. "And I will do what I have to."

At first glance it seemed Tony had garroted himself while lying down flat on his back. One end of a leather thong— probably a contraband shoelace—was coiled around his neck. The other end was clutched in Tony's right hand, which hung rigidly at his side. There were no other marks of struggle. Suspiciously, there was no sign of any death throws. No gasping or vomiting. No contorted face. It appeared Tony had administered a quick and lethal snap to his own neck. Was that physically possible in this position?

After Brocard had said a few prayers for the poor boy's soul and anointed him with chrism, he began to search for a note, something to indicate why Tony might have done something so drastic, so terribly stupid. Under the mattress he found what he was looking for: a page on which was scrawled a strange catalogue of places and people, under the title The Web. He gave it a swift read, knowing Officer Thomas and company would descent on him. It read:

> Heroin from Burma Buddha to Pennsy Amish;
> Crack from PR Santería to Harlem Five-Percenters;
> Cigarettes from Bible Belt to Bible City;
> Caravaggio from Sicilian Catholics to Zurich Zwinglis.

The Amish, Santería, the Bible Belt, and Caravaggio: If it was gibberish, it was so compulsively written and carefully constructed as to constitute a new category of delusional behavior.

Brocard slipped the note into his pocket just as the officers entered the cell.

"Jesus! Excuse me, Father," the lieutenant said. "How long has this fucker been dead?" Then, seeing that rigor mortis had long since set in, he began to berate Thomas and anyone else within shouting distance. Saying that he would be glad to be of help if needed—"Just call"—Father Brocard slipped away from the Ad Seg Unit.

What on earth could Caravaggio have to do with this prison? *Then again,* he thought, his face lighting up at the prospect, *whom better to encounter in such a place?*

Five

"RECIDIVISM," SHE SAID WITH AN AUTHORITY that could not be broached. "Recidivism, Father Brocard, is what it is all about."

Given the gravity of the situation—an inmate was dead after all, and murder could not be ruled out—it was not unreasonable to expect the warden to stop, for once, her interminable lecturing. But Tamara Boggs had worked hard for her degree—Lord, had she worked hard—and it had become her life's work to convince others that she was an educated woman, worthy of the lofty position of authority to which Prison World Inc. had raised her. Of course, it never crossed her mind that her intransigence and her susceptibility to certain forms of flattery made her the perfect toady. Fortunately for her, if for no one else, the truth seldom if ever reared its ugly head at Brotherly Love Pen.

"There are some people who think that the policies I have set in place here are too lax," the warden continued. Was this perhaps her way of sliding into the subject at hand? Brocard could only hope. "But studies show—Matthews and Pitt provide a good example—that if positive programs are offered and if the program's integrity…" At this she trailed off, as if backing away from a concept too large for her to grasp securely. Or perhaps she had simply lost her train of thought. "That is what is so important," she said firmly, "to keep a program's integrity."

"About the dead body in Ad Seg." Brocard could see no subtle way of introducing the subject. "I think—"

"I am pleased by your concern, Father Brocard," she interrupted. He could see very clearly that she was not. A very unladylike mustache of sweat glistened on her upper lip. "The chief is already on top of this. Reports are being drawn up and the social worker has already told Tony's parents about his suicide."

Increasingly annoyed at the warden's refusal to talk candidly about the event in Cell 13, Brocard changed the topic to something about which he could legitimately complain. "I feel that, as chaplain, I should have been consulted about notifying the parents. I am schooled in this you know." Death, in his past monastic life, had been a commonplace. He had long since lost track of how many he had either buried or consoled.

The warden regarded Brocard disdainfully. "Maybe in the future we can put a policy in place where the chaplains work together with the social workers at times like this. It is a policy that will have to come from the top. No promises. As you probably are aware, statistics have shown that deaths inside our jail are extremely rare."

Does that mean, Brocard wondered maliciously, *that they are only reported in the ambulance rushing corpses to the hospital?* He could not help but feel that Warden Boggs had been schooled in how to avoid any topic that might negatively impact on Prison World Inc. That was one lesson she had managed to learn well. He could neither walk out of her office nor bear to listen to her twaddle a moment longer. So he let his eyes and mind wander freely while the warden continued to issue feckless orders and offer meaningless excuses.

What struck him about both Tamara Boggs and her spacious

office was how consciously all personal touches had been avoided. None of those gilded plaques or dried flowers or Hallmark statuettes of golfers that one might have expected to find in the office of someone who had risen so far so fast. Most tellingly of all, there were no family photos anywhere to be seen. A lesbian, Brocard concluded. Well, there was *one* thing he liked about her, at least. Now, as for her sense of style: that left something to be desired.

Warden Boggs had helmet hair, surprising for a woman in her mid 40s, even more so in a woman of color. Why would she go to all that trouble? Being almost completely bald, Brocard could see no charm in hair torture. And for her clothes: padded shoulders? Even a monk wouldn't make that mistake.

"If we continue increasing viable programs…" she prattled on. As he focused more intently on her, she mistook the nature of Brocard's interest and began to hurl criminal-justice speak at him with increased ferocity. The phrase "null hypothesis" puffed out her plump cheeks, while "standard deviation" emphasized the fullness and unusual purplish hue of her lips. *As if there ever were anything like "standard deviation,"* Brocard thought. Not in his world. As the warden purred "mean, median, and mode," she leaned forward in almost feline fashion. Not a bad looker in her own way. No doubt Zinka would know what to do with her.

Zinka! Why hadn't he thought of her sooner? She would surely know whether there was any connection between Caravaggio, Sicily, and Zurich. And in her own inimitable way, she would know what to make of Warden Boggs and the boys at Brotherly Love. But how to get her in? It was obvious Tamara was not about to allow a murder investigation to cramp the enlightened style of her model jail. But her precious uplift programs might be the key.

Brocard interrupted her lecture to ask her, "Is there any way we might bring some helpful program into the Chapel? Not necessarily religious, perhaps, but something positive for the inmates?" He was playing by her rules now and, having no idea what he was really up to, she foolishly thought she had finally worn him down.

"Yes, I see," she said excitedly. "Something like the Howard League proposals might have a salutary impact." Where that came from, Brocard couldn't say. Warden Boggs was beside herself.

"Behavior modification," she mused. "No doubt about it." Looking at her expectantly, hoping this might be the opening he needed, he waited for her to explain. "It's a relatively straight-forward program. We studied it in graduate school. Many prisons have already initiated it. There is a handbook: Everything is spelled out."

"Could I perhaps look for some volunteers to run it?" Brocard ventured.

"What a helpful idea. Money is at a premium these days. And actually almost anyone can run it as long as they have a calm, relaxed way about them."

Zinka to a tee, Brocard thought rather maliciously.

As the warden held forth about the handbook and exemplary effects of behavior mod, Brocard looked down to see the crumpled page he still clutched in his hand. He concluded it was best not to mention Tony Polluto's note. Tampering with evidence and all that. Anyway, something told him the good warden, intent on her job more than anything else, would just file it away in the shredder.

Brocard's heart began to race as he thought about Zinka. It had been so long since they solved *St. Agatha's* mystery. Where on earth had that curious woman gotten to?

Six

THE DEVIL WAS NO ABSTRACT CONSTRUCT. No quaint medieval remnant, hanging around to enliven our literature or tweak our interest in the seamier side of life. No, for Father Avertanus Deblaer, retired from teaching but never from thinking about the metaphysical, the devil was palpable, someone to be avoided if possible but fearlessly confronted if necessary. In fact, he had assisted at several exorcisms during his active ministry. They had been harrowing experiences that had taken their toll on his otherwise pacific nature. In light of this, what puzzled him most about his old friend Brocard was that, after all they had experienced together, seen with their own eyes, he still seemed incapable of accepting the reality of the devil.

One time his compadre Father Malachi, a satanologist of international repute, had asked him to witness the final stage of the removal of a spirit. As anyone conversant with such things knows, evil loves to haunt certain godforsaken places, where it lodges as a parasite in the unfortunate body of anyone who fails to keep his guard. A young, naive priest, unaware of the evil place around him—or perhaps just too cavalier about it—got caught in the grips of the Evil One. The violence of the contortions, the unbelievable physical disfigurement the possessed had to endure were things Father Avertanus would never forget. Nor should he.

And there was Brocard, E-mailing him about some ill-begotten scheme to retrieve stolen art and to solve the mystery of one, possibly even two murders in a prison, of all places: the favorite haunt of Beelzebub. Even more distressing was Brocard's tone. Breathless bits of incomplete sentences—not unlike a schoolgirl's talk.

Praying over how to proceed, Avertanus realized this was not the time to lecture, to become haughty, or worse still, pious. He always had to fight that tendency. No, the best thing was to give Brocard the information he requested and to monitor the situation closely.

Zinka, that strange caricature of a woman, still largely the man she had been before the operation and hormones, had spent the past several months traveling between her old home in Rome and new flat in Paris. All of her activity had to do with the series of Poussin paintings she had authenticated. Of which *St. Agatha,* Brocard always had to remind himself, was but one. As she began to establish herself as a world-class art historian, Zinka sensed the signs of strain in her relationship with Camille, her sedate librarian companion. It wasn't that they didn't still love each other, Zinka assured Avertanus in their regular correspondence during those months. They just seemed to be going in different directions. Paris was where her heart and fashionable body longed to be. Rome seemed far too sleepy and, well, passé. Zinka could not understand why it was impossible for Camille, Parisian to the core, to move back to Paris, even though her overbearing parents were still there. Obnoxious they were, but no more so than most people in Zinka's estimation. "Maybe, someday," Camille would say, hoping her parents would finally move out to the country. Maybe then there would finally be space for another Blanchierdarie on Avenue Foch.

Then, as fate would have it, Zinka and Camille had a run of good luck. In one of those frequent fog-bound multiple-car crashes on a motorway in the Loire Valley, both of Camille's parents were smashed as flat as pancakes. When he received the news, Avertanus had been struck by the visual anomaly of such massive human carnage in the midst of such natural and man-made beauty. He did so love the châteaux of the Loire and promised himself to make it down to Chambord at least one more time. After her initial and extremely short-lived shock, Camille realized that God had spoken. The flat in Paris was now theirs and, presumably, their relationship would finally be restored to its old, lustrous, lustful state. Zinka, on her part, could not stop thinking about the closets full of clothes that the mother of all clotheshorses had left behind. Granted, the shoes would take some shoving into, but the scarves alone were worth the hurried move.

And so it was that the E-mail address Brocard tracked down for Zinka went through to her apartment in Paris. What he could not have realized was how bored and sad she was. Until, that is, she heard from her old friend. His news was to change everything.

Seven

"Your tits sag, Camille!"

There was, of course, no delicate way for Zinka to say this. Nevertheless, her words seemed particularly hurtful today. Just when their spirits were rising, just when some hope of escaping their *haut bourgeois* malaise had finally come, a domestic squabble blew in like a squall. Both of them wondered whether they would ever find peace.

Camille scowled at her bosom. "They were always pert and firm in Rome, *n'est-ce pas?*" She sidled warily toward the dressing mirror, turning slightly in profile to inspect her breasts. "Ever since we moved to Paris they have begun to, how do you say, 'snag'?"

"Sag," Zinka said softly, moving close to her and gently taking Camille's tiny deflated breasts in her enormous hands. She flashed on an image of King Kong with Fay Wray, then quickly banished it. Not a helpful thought. "And don't blame lovely Paris, my little melon." She was trying oh-so-hard to be a healer. But compassion was never her strong suit, even at best of times. "You *are* nearly 50, after all."

As Camille attempted to protest, Zinka opened her mouth, and in her irrepressible Slavic way, stopped Camille in her tracks with brute force. With her breasts and thighs she pinned her lover against the mirror. Her lips parted and locked over those of her willing partner, who was no longer troubled by her pooped *poitrine*. But when Zinka came up for air, reality set in again. How sad. Life had been so simple without bras, which to Zinka were as sure a sign of senescence as dentures.

"Just put it on." Zinka held out the Victoria's Secret uplift special—the seed of the whole nasty incident—with a triumphant air. "There is no way we're going to Fouquet's with your titties anything but proud and pretty."

"Well, we'll see," Camille said glumly. She shoved her arms through the straps like a teenage girl fumbling with her first brassiere, her back to the mirror lest she become embarrassed. Zinka motioned for her to turn around and made sure the contraption was fastened securely. Zinka paid no mind to Camille's protestations: She realized that, most probably, Camille was also getting off on this new fetish object. What would Camille Paglia think? Women love toys as much as boys.

Camille's bra on and her tits in place, Zinka could finally display her excitement over the real matter of the moment: Brocard's E-mail about men in prison, a murder or two, and—almost too good to be true—a Caravaggio nativity: lost, stolen, fake, no matter. There were mysteries to be solved.

It was a short stroll from their apartment on Foch over to Avenue Georges V and up to Fouquet's on the corner of the Champs Elysées. Being in the *seizième arrondissement*, that most exalted of Parisian *quartiers*, Zinka never took for granted. One never knew whom one might pass or who might be looking from behind parted curtains. Even the buildings have eyes in the *seizième*. With all the planets apparently aligned in their favor, they proceeded with such style, that, had Zinka been less Amazonian in stature and more discreet in apparel, one might have thought two royals— two queens for that matter—had deigned to visit the *quartier à pied.*

Once they were ensconced at their favorite table, the one on the corner in full view of *tout le Paris,* and after they had placed their order, Zinka pulled a hard copy of Father Brocard's E-mail from her purse. Her hand trembled as she read excerpts.

"'My very dearest Zinka'—honestly, Camille, I never thought timid little Brocard was that fond of me. Always thought I— well, how can I put it?" Zinka always tried extra hard to be demure. "I always thought I overwhelmed him a bit." Brushing back her hair and pushing out her massive bust, she forged on. No one or nothing could stop her now. "'If we are to solve this, I need your help on two fronts. First, I must know if there is a Sicilian *Caravaggio* missing.'"

Camille thought the whole thing too absurd but deferred to Zinka's enthusiasm as she read on. "'Then, if there is a painting to be found, I will need you here with me in prison. I have a plan. Don't worry, you will be perfectly safe.'" Zinka wanted to say, "It's those cute little inmates who should worry!" But for once she kept her thoughts to herself. This was no time to alienate her little librarian lover.

Then, seizing Camille in a most unladylike way, she proclaimed "Zinka is back!"

Eight

SOME PEOPLE WERE JUST MEANT TO HAVE DOORS opened for them, and Zinka Pavlic was blissfully happy to count herself among them. How many years, trapped in the body of the man she never wanted to be, had she held the door open for women, all the while envying their feeling of exaltation? She fantasized how wondrous and empowering it would be to have the opposite sex bow and scrape before her. This gnawing desire alone—and there were so many others—would have been enough to compel her to take a knife to those extraneous genitals. Now that she was a woman, she bristled at the feminist attack on all such gender privileges. This absurd assault on civility was certainly not as virulent in France as in the States, but it was a disturbing trend nevertheless.

And since her precipitous rise to fame in the art world, doors of a more figurative kind had also sprung open for Zinka. Now, with Camille in tow, she glided regally from the taxi hailed for them at Fouquet's into the administration foyer of the Louvre in the Carré Napoléon. A sharply dressed young assistant whisked them past faceless supernumeraries into the small but well-appointed office of Zinka's dear friend Dr. Emile Rothenburg, director emeritus of painting.

"Emile," she said, quite pleased that they were on first name basis, "a tantalizing prospect has come my way. A mystery, *dis donc,* that I hope you can help solve."

Dr. Rothenburg, who loathed being called Emile by anyone except his senile mother, was—if the truth be known—filled with gas. Always a corpulent gourmand, the combination of retirement and late-in-life fame (not just Téléfrance but even Diane Sawyer had interviewed him over the Poussin discovery) had pushed him over the edge into gluttony. He had neglected to kiss Doctor Pavlic's hand not because he was too large to leave his seat without a modest bit of struggle. And, to be sure, a passionate man of his advanced years would never turn down a chance to inspect so formidable a bosom as Zinka possessed. No, it was simply that he had a kielbasa in his hand, discreetly concealed under this desk but as spicy and forthright as it could possibly be. Those Central Europeans certainly knew their meats.

Observant Camille knew that Doctor Rothenberg had heard nothing Zinka had said. Moreover, she could not help wondering at the weight he had put on these past few months. He had become a positively mountainous creature. In her trim and disciplined little body, she could only marvel at his prodigious, if deadly, accomplishment.

After a second false start, the eminent curator emeritus rallied. Covertly placing the cherished sausage in a desk drawer, he got on board.

"There has always been speculation that several key Cara-vaggios are out there in attics and chapels, just waiting to be dis-covered," he began. "The Dublin *Betrayal of Jesus* is an *exemple parfait.*" Rising slightly from his chair and assuming his profes-sorial mode, Dr. Rothenberg settled in for the long haul. "In her recent work, Helen Langdon, in a popular style but with such sterling research, maintains there are several key missing works which she thinks might soon surface. I must say I agree. Perhaps—"

"No lectures, Emile, please," Zinka interjected. "I have a good friend, Father Brocard, you remember, who is, as we speak, hunkered down with rapists and murders. He is embroiled in some conspiracy. Bodies are piling up, Emile! They are piling up! So let's get to work here."

Camille lowered her eyes and sank even lower into her chair. How could Zinka be so assertive here in the Louvre? In the face of ancient tradition and social imperatives? Imagine: telling a state employee, a dignitary of such rank, to get to work. Unthinkable.

"A Nativity," the Doctor muttered as Zinka's words began to sink in. "A Nativity, did you say?" He spoke like a man coming out of a deep sleep. "Did you say a Nativity from Sicily?"

As he buzzed his secretary to have her bring in the appropriate Interpol folders, Dr. Emile Rothenberg's whole being changed. He was his old self again, focused and assured.

"It can't be!" he exclaimed as he rifled the files. Then, looking at Zinka he realized anything was possible. "Back in 1969, one of his last great works was stolen from the Oratory of San Lorenzo. The case is still open on what has become commonly known as the elusive *Palermo Caravaggio*."

Nine

HE COULD FEEL THE RED TRAVELING UP HIS NECK into his cheeks and rising inexorably above his forehead to the broad swath of his bald pate. This was not the way it was meant to be. A sprinkling of holy water, a turn up the aisle with the aspergillum, a splash to the left, then one to the right. It should have been so meaningful. Well, if not meaningful, at least solemn. But solemnity was scarce in jail.

Despite the circumstances, Brocard insisted on doing as near a proper Mass as possible once a week. After all, everything was there for him when he arrived. All the vestments and liturgical paraphernalia, from cruets to monstrance. And, being Roman-trained, he had a longing as deep as the sea for doing things right.

The problem was his congregation, which often gave new meaning to the expression "unchurched." With the rarest of exceptions, the poor boys didn't have a clue. He had to tell them when to stand and when to kneel. He even took the time to explain why he was doing what he was doing—just one step shy of show-and-tell. And when it came to unusual whistles and bells, like this ritual sprinkling with holy water, confusion bordering on chaos often reigned. Only the handful of Filipinos kept quiet—not that they were any more clearheaded than the Hispanics and Anglos.It was just their way. Everyone else buzzed with questions and succumbed easily to the air of hilarity.

Cuchifrito didn't help. As self-appointed choir director, pianist, and cantor, he labored mightily to support Father Brocard's liturgical needs. But, as is so often the case, good intentions and ability are rarely equally matched. Granted, Brocard should have prepared him to play some appropriate music to accompany the liturgical sprinkling. And Brocard should have seen in Cuchifrito's panicked eyes that "Just play some music while I sprinkle" was not even remotely computing. But who could have imagined he would decide to play—and more distressingly to sing—"The Star-Spangled Banner"? Father Brocard, fully vested and trying hard to be dignified, paraded through a chapel full of hardened criminals while Cuchifrito threw himself into the national anthem as only a Dominicano with rhythm and an evil falsetto could do.

Suddenly, in one of those reversals so common at Brotherly Love Pen, Brocard noticed that the chapel had fallen eerily quiet. Everyone seemed to be waiting either for more water or, more probably, for Cuchifrito's last bloodcurdling notes. The diminutive pianist, a favorite with many inmates for reasons Brocard chose not to think about, rose from the piano and threw his little heart into an a cappella "bombs bursting in air." Then just as suddenly, the silence was broken by applause. Not just tepid applause but rather that ear-splitting, board-thumping, screech-filled applause that those who have never been told better are capable of.

"Water," Brocard began his homily as the applause subsided. "Water," he said again, as much to silence his congregation as for dramatic effect. "Water connects all of us. Every one of us here, everyone on the planet, is two-thirds water."

He could see that he had caught Dean's attention. T-Rex—the black guy with scaly skin and extremely short arms—seemed also to be with him. The other 100 or so would catch up, he hoped.

"We Christians are connected by water. All Christians are baptized in water, but we are not alone in our need for water." He saw a couple of the Hispanic guys move closer to each other— some even put their arms around the young men next to them. Why weren't the Anglos that friendly? "All religions in all times have used water to bring people together and to help them to strengthen their faith."

Awkwardly said. Brocard knew he could do better if he weren't so preoccupied with looking out for mischief makers in the chapel. He had heard that the chapel, one of the few places where inmates could gather unsupervised, was a haven for gangs and a convenient place for drug and pornography drops. But he still found this news hard to believe. He would wager there was more good in his congregation than evil. And that for many of these inmates, this was a place to change, to get well.

A couple of black guys smirked when Brocard mentioned our collective need to purify ourselves—to die to our willfulness and to be born anew. These hardened men known as Five-Percenters believed they were beyond other human beings. In their own minds they were gods themselves, with no need of any white man's construct. Brocard felt like striking out at them. But he was above ad hominem attacks. At least for the moment. He already felt prison life beginning to wear down his restraint. And he knew that the breaking point would come sooner rather than later. For now, he let them be and continued his preaching.

"Mark describes Jesus's baptism in an almost apocalyptic way." Now he had lost them. Words too long, a concept too big to grasp. He tried again. "Mark writes as if the world is coming to an end. Not because it is, but because we have to act as if it is." He could see he was really getting through to Dean, who was leaning toward him, intent on blocking out the noise around him to hear what Brocard had to say. And he caught sight of Jesucito raising his hands and swaying. A bit too Pentecostal for Brocard's taste, but a sign he was listening.

"The Kingdom of God, as John the Baptizer reminds us, is at hand. Now is the time to change, to turn our backs on our sinfulness and to turn towards Jesus Christ."

By now Jesucito was standing and flailing his arms about. As was Cuchifrito, never one to be upstaged. Although Brocard had not finished his sermon, he thought it best to end right there. After all, this was the congregation that had just responded with a standing ovation to "The Star-Spangled Banner." Hardly a demanding orthodox bunch. No, Brocard thought it best to go straight into the Prayers of the Faithful. Half the chapel was standing by now, anyway.

This, together with the Kiss of Peace, was the part of the Mass the inmates seemed to like the most. They could speak freely about their needs and wants, could openly mention people and situations they wanted prayers for. Even though it always disintegrated into rowdiness, Brocard considered this time essential to the prisoners' prayer life and never once considered omitting spontaneous prayers from the service. Until it was too late.

"And for what else should we pray?" Brocard asked his charges.

One inmate, another whose limbs were too short for his torso, waved his stunted little arms and spoke over a couple of fainter voices. "I want to pray for the mother of my child who is crazy— you know, crazy. She's sick, too."

Brocard signaled the congregation's response with "Let us pray to the Lord."

Then, after the usual welter of complaints and petitions, Dean spoke up. His voice was trembling and filled with emotion, but clear enough for all to hear.

"For Tony. He shouldn't have had to die. Tony didn't deserve to die. I want to pray he doesn't meet the real devil—that he isn't in hell."

Until that moment, Brocard had never considered Dean a suspect. Was guilt getting to him? Did he have opportunity? Motive? As the priest pondered these possibilities, Jesucito launched into his mandatory prayer against the *demonio,* equally inarticulate in Spanish and English. Perhaps, Brocard thought, it was time to spend a late night at Brotherly Love Pen and see what really happens after hours.

As he and the congregation stood in prayer, Andy peered into the chapel through a crack in the sliding smoked-plastic doors. Brocard could see him there. Andy was observing but not entering, as he often did. It struck Brocard as curious that Andy never entered during services. The explanation he offered when Brocard questioned him—that he was unsure of his own faith— never rang true. Still, he was a good worker and, for the time being, indispensable.

If Brocard had looked deeper into the truth at this early stage, he might have saved himself much grief. But who among us ever gets the timing right in matters of fate?

Ten

HE WAS AN UNLIKELY GUIDE: AN INMATE PLUMBER with a brain the size of a muskrat's. But Cavallo had many qualities to recommend him. First, he had a rather amazing ponytail, which he displayed dramatically like a proud Lipizzaner. He was, in other words, easy to spot at a distance or in a crowd. Second, as the plumber in a facility constantly in need of repair, he was called everywhere to patch leaks and unclog drains. Especially on third shift when, because staff was off duty and officers were unfailingly weary, Brotherly Love Pen was the domain of its inmates. In the wee hours, Cavallo was the only show in town. Of course, Brocard had no way of knowing what kind of show Cavallo produced, but, growing more worldly by the hour, he had his suspicions.

Third, Cavallo was hung like a horse. Would there were a more dignified way of putting it. But in such matters, decorum must give way to directness. If rulers were allowed in jail, the general population and custody alike would have had proof positive that Cavallo's was no common endowment. Over 10 inches long and—the mind boggled —half a foot in circumference when fully erect. Which, more often than not, it was.

Rumor had it that when he was in the county jail, before he was sent down to Brotherly Love, he had found someone to service him. That was just the kind of guy Cavallo was.

Only having penetrated women to that point, and surely having no idea what damage he might do to the owner of an overly anxious and ill-prepared rectum, Cavallo soon discovered that the bunghole lacks the obliging elasticity of a vagina. A hole by any other name is not just a hole. Despite the increasingly shrill protestations of his initially enthusiastic receptor, he had shoved and pushed and finally ripped the poor boy apart. Blood, mayhem, and the cops were everywhere. This event assured him not only a sterling prison reputation but also a healthy respect for what hung between his legs.

"Word is bond," Cavallo solemnly intoned to the priest.

"Pardon?" Much as he tried, Father Brocard had still not perfected prison-speak. There was so much to learn about his new metalanguage. "Does that mean you promise not to tell anyone I will be periodically making these covert rounds?"

"Word *is* bond." Cavallo could not believe Brocard was so out of touch. Since years of recreational drug use had deprived him of all long-term memories. This was the only world Cavallo knew, and prison-speak was the only language he really knew. There were no other references. "Word *is* bond," he said again firmly. At that, both inmate and priest decided to drop the matter.

"Well, that's good," Brocard mumbled as he followed the bouncing mane and Cavallo's wheelcart of plungers down the main corridor and out into the quadrangle. The night air was piercing, so cold that snow and ice could not form. Even cold enough to keep inmates from peering from their windows to whistle their approval as Cavallo passed. Tonight garbage bags sealed all the windows to shut out drafts as well as light and noise, which made the jail more sinisterly dark and still than usual. All signs augured ill for Brocard's incipient investigation. Still, there were always things to learn about this strange new world. Buoyed by the optimism priests so often have, Brocard knew he would not come up empty-handed.

"In here," Cavallo grunted as he roughly nudged Brocard into a vacant social worker's office just by the entrance to East House. Brocard wondered where the guard was. Why the gate was open to the tier was even more of a mystery.

As Brocard slipped into the bleak closet of a room and partially closed the door, he wondered whether his horny guide was taking his role just a little too seriously. But just then he saw Dean pass by carrying what looked like a sheaf of papers. Better to proceed unobserved. That was the plan and Cavallo was right to take it seriously. How strange: It was 10 o'clock at night, and all the inmates were supposedly locked down, yet Dean wandered the corridors with impunity.

"Oh, there you are," a gruff voice said, shattering the silence. "Get your ass into Cell 15. Room's open. Toilet's not working. Move it."

Even the meanest felon had a healthy fear of Kraus, the third shift sergeant. However, to Brocard, Eurocentric to the core, the officer's thick German accent had a lilt to it that could only mean the South and, more hopefully still, Catholic.

"Bavaria?" he queried, thinking it best not to mention why he had taken refuge in the open office. Brocard had the free range of the institution, he was always told. What better time to see whether that were true. "Munich perhaps?"

"Just outside." She went from Stollen to a cream puff in an instant. And as proof she signaled for Brocard to sit next to her at the guard desk. "How clever you are, Father."

After obligatory talk about beer and schnitzel, Father Brocard asked, as discreetly as possible, why an inmate like Dean should be allowed to wander, seemingly at will, when others were locked down. The answer was not very settling.

"Who knows why any of dis crap is happening?" was Kraus's reply. She followed up with complaints about cost-cutting and the shortage of officers. Furthermore, most of the officers, especially during the graveyard shift, were completely unqualified and unreliable. "Who de hell ever herds of a sergeant sitting dis post anyway?" What's more, certain inmates had cards issued because of their jobs, which allowed them mobility even at night. "Dat shouldn't be, Father."

"Can Dean get into the Ad Seg Unit?" Brocard wondered.

"Dat one, he gets anywhere. Makes me sick," Kraus lamented. Then, returning to the question at hand, she explained, "He's one of Officer Thomas's boys."

"But Thomas is second shift, I thought."

"He's too much in debt to leave ever. When he does, he's down in A.C. for a few hours at de tables. Den back on de post. He holds da record for overtime," Kraus said with a mirthless chuckle.

"What about all of his born-again religion? His Bible-thumping?"

"Bullshit," Kraus spat. Then, worrying she might have gone too far, she corrected herself as best she knew how. "Excuse me, Father. 'Shit' I mean. No bullshit. Don't get to talk to priests down here too often." Then, seething still, "Just can't stand no bullshitting phonies."

Working her way carefully around the language barrier between them, Kraus said she hoped that Father wasn't planning on waiting for Cavallo to unplug the toilet in Cell 15 because, as only she could put it, "Dey is waiting two deep to give him blow jobs."

"I thought there was a clogged toilet to repair," Brocard replied, wide-eyed.

"Father," she said, in an almost patronizing tone, "why do you think they jam socks down their toilets after 10 o'clock every night?" It became clear that in her own gruff way, Officer Kraus was motherly at heart. "Got to allow the boys some fun."

Then an idea came to Brocard. One that time and opportunity seemed to allow.

"When you think Dean will be gone for a while," he began, "and if you would be able to help me, would it be possible to see what he has in his room?" Then, realizing this was too vague, he added. "I have reason to believe he might be hiding things missing from the chapel."

"A fucking swag," Kraus snorted. Her eyes lit up brighter than Oktoberfest at the very thought. Brocard was thankful that "swag," room search in prison talk, was, *mirabile dictu,* one of the new words in his vocabulary.

As everyone in East House was single-bunked, there was nothing to do but simply tear the place to bits. Brocard was impressed by Kraus's determination as he ran to follow her down the hall. Groans and sucking noises drew Brocard's attention to Cell 15, where he caught a brief glimpse of Cavallo's naked body. The inmate's arms stretched up to grasp a plunger stuck to the ceiling. "For balance," Kraus muttered.

What a professional Sergeant Kraus proved to be. Not an envelope went unopened, not a crevice uninspected. She was not particularly neat, of course, but that never was the objective of a thorough swag. Just look for anything out of place. And occasionally, if nothing turns up but a charge must be pinned on the inmate, plant something. Prison justice, but it worked.

As papers flew and clothes lay strewn about, Brocard picked up an unfamiliar Bible marked Moody. When opened, a photograph flew out onto the floor. A shiver went through him as he bent to pick it up. He almost shouted to Kraus to stop what she was doing. Father Brocard had found what he was looking for. But, because Kraus obviously loved to swag, he let her continue with her fun.

Eleven

My dear Zinka,

God willing, I can get this scanner to work and E-mail you the photograph that I found earlier tonight during a search of an inmate's room. To my unschooled eye, it looks like a Caravaggio. Lots of shadows and an impressive angel virtually swooping into your face. Excuse me, there has to be a better way of saying this. I am beginning to sound like an inmate. Have patience with me. Should you get here, and I trust that this photograph is enough to lure you over, you will see what I mean. This world has its way of rubbing off on one. Anyway, I have had my suspicions about this inmate for some time. He wears his religion, such as it is, very heavily. And past experiences have shown people like that to be the most devious. Perhaps I am jumping to conclusions, but I think he is our man.

Well, dear Zinka, it is three in the morning. The rectory is quiet as a tomb, but then again so is Bryn Mawr and the entire Main Line. People of means seem to know how to set limits on themselves. Having no means myself and being a nervous type by nature, I have no such discipline. Please let me know soon if you get the photograph. It should come as an attachment to this E-mail. But you probably know that already. Download it, or whatever they call it, and do let me know if this is our Caravaggio. I anxiously await your news.

—Brocard

"No discipline!" Zinka called out to Camille in the other room.

"Yes, dear, I know," Camille replied with a sigh.

"Not me, my moist little melon." Camille had learned to put aside her natural aversion to both endearments and alliteration. At least Zinka was happy again, which meant that they might be happy again, together. She hurried into the library to see what all the excitement was about.

"Precious little Brocard says he has no discipline." Zinka was positively beside herself with glee. "That little monk doesn't know a thing about laxity and irresponsibility."

"Well, you certainly could teach him a thing or two about depravity," Camille retorted. She did try—God knows she tried—but her attempts at humor really did not go over. Faced with an indignant stare from her imperious girlfriend, Camille decided to let Zinka have fun all by herself—and hoped against hope that some of it might spill over from her to Brocard. He did so need to lighten up. Even Camille, turgid little soul that she was, could see that.

"Download and let's see what we've got," Zinka said to the computer as the bits of the photograph of the *Palermo Caravaggio* assembled on the monitor.

Camille pulled a Venetian slipper chair to the desk and, resorting to the well-brought-up mode, took her seat, folded her hands, and breathed very shallowly.

"Hold on, baby. This is the big one," Zinka moaned with feline delight. She placed both hands on the desk, threw back her head, and slowly raised her impressive body out of the chair. Arms outstretched and hips swaying to a tune that she alone could hear, she groaned, "Yes." And one more time: "Yes." And for dramatic effect, "Yes, yes, yes."

Camille wondered less about what this signified than how on earth Zinka had acquired such a strangely colloquial and almost American way of speaking. Was it the fault of Sky TV, with those late night programs from places like Burbank that her girlfriend soaked in? Or was it sadly the product of her interaction with some ill-begotten chat group? Was Zinka in touch with some Valley creature perhaps? There was no way of telling.

"This is it, my little pumpkin," Zinka purred, "The *Palermo Caravaggio*." Then, crouching as far down to her as her tight little skirt would allow—she always had to make allowances for those massive quadriceps she had developed in the army—she directed Camille's attention to the picture that filled the screen. "See the plunging angel bearing the traditional banderole GLORIA IN EXCELSIS DEO and then that mournful, pitiful Nativity. Splendid. This is a baby Jesus just one small step from the grave."

Although Camille found it hard to get excited about the prospect of another caper, with the heady smell and sexy bulk of the woman she loved bearing down on her, how could she complain?

Twelve

DEATH WAS SUCH A TIDY AFFAIR IN HOLLAND. Maybe it was the compactness of the landscape, or perhaps a congenital anal retentiveness endemic to the society. Whatever the reason, the orderly disposal of mortal remains had a profoundly settling and even calming effect on Father Avertanus. This was even more so when the corpse in question (today, Celestine, the sacristan from hell) belonged to someone who in life had been unremittingly unpleasant. It was always good to see such a person meet a fitting end. How wonderful to know that another boor had been silenced forever.

Death, Avertanus reflected as he made his way from the community cemetery to his cell, was truly at his heels. Time was creeping up on him. But the steady march of death was inevitable in the nursing-home monastery where he lived. It seemed that, as soon as they filled one hole, the gravediggers were opening another. He needed no skull on his desk as a memento mori. All he had to do was to dine with the brothers: Death lingered over every meal like an unwanted guest.

Still, scholar that he was, he had better things to obsess over. This sticky business with his old friend Brocard, for example. Not the dead bodies and the *Caravaggio*. Those were issues that concerned him little. No, it was the curious reference to the Moody Bible that had sent him scurrying to the library to research once more for his old friend. And to consider as well how wise it was that Brocard had not shut him out. On the contrary, Brocard had assiduously maintained contact with Avertanus, knowing that not to do so might set him adrift, untethering him forever from tradition and authority. A risk too dangerous for anyone of a Catholic bent to take.

Theirs was as strange a relationship as their very names: Brocard and Avertanus. Names given by a religious order at a time when such things were common—names that set them apart from the world. Time and place, not personality or interest, connected them. They had both been stationed at the Monastery of San Redempto in Rome for more years than either of them could remember, and both had been molded by the grinding rhythm of monastic life. But whereas Brocard, the practical brother, showed himself to be a master of details; Avertanus, the community's reigning scholar, displayed an extraordinary facility in metaphysics and mystical theology: realms in which Brocard never dared to tread.

In many ways, Avertanus *was* embodiment of the old order, hierarchical and systematically structured. Clinging to their friendship even after the monastery was gone had allowed Brocard to grow in ways he couldn't have, if he had simply yielded to the temptation to sever ties with his past. Breaking with the past is never the tonic we hope for. Regrets remain and issues go unresolved. Reconciling the present with the past makes life full and meaningful. And despite his eccentricities and his reactionary insights, Brocard was grateful still to have wise old Father Avertanus in his life.

Avertanus, too, was grateful: not to have been discarded, first of all—younger people often forget their mentors when they move on and change interests. Grateful that Brocard still seemed to need his help, if only to check facts and sound out his opinions. In truth, no students contacted Avertanus any more, although he had taught hundreds over his years at the Gregorian. Granted, he did offer spiritual direction to visitors who asked him for it. But the effort was increasingly perfunctory, lacking the struggle of Christian life as he knew it. Now, as for the life behind bars Brocard had chosen: that rivaled the lives of the Desert Fathers, who had known nothing but danger and who had survived solely on grace. Brocard brought to Avertanus's life a sense that the old ways, the old faith, had not been completely abandoned.

In this respect it was Avertanus who needed Brocard more, at least at this stage in their friendship. Through Brocard, Avertanus escaped the gloom of the house of death to which his religious community had relegated him, and found something challenging and new to think about. What more could he ask of any friend? What greater favor could he want?

Fortunately, Avertanus's trip to the library yielded a bounty of information. Another part of the riddle unraveled, and more significantly, another sign of their friendship and mutual need appeared, disguised as it was in a simple E-mail.

Your casual reference to a Moody Bible in the cell of the deceased inmate made my head swim. How exotic your life must be at that prison! I have only read about and trembled at, I must say, these aberrant religious beliefs that continent of yours has spawned. The Moody Institute, as it grandly calls itself, is part of the cluster of unrest-inducing fundamentalist religions that gather around what is known as the Evangelical Revival. They are fearmongers, my brother. They hate Catholics with a passion and long for the destruction of all except the few chosen ones, among whom they number themselves. Be careful, my brother. The devil chooses many guises—most commonly, as I am sure you are aware, the one of piety.

Thirteen

"TELL ME THAT ISN'T PRETTY?"

The question was rhetorical, as is often the case with completely self-involved creatures. But, were Brocard to have answered, he would have had to admit that Dean the Nose was an attractive man. In this case, the mirror that held Dean's gaze told no lies. Though Brocard distrusted Dean fully and knew there was surely some ulterior motive for his visit, the priest allowed him the luxury of a quick preen, all the while marveling at how unobservant he had been.

Surely Dean's chiseled cowboy look and the impressive musculature that even his prison browns could not hide were as much a part of who he was as his belief system or con games. Especially at Brotherly Love Pen, where looks parlayed into favors and favors into power. What Brocard also should have noticed was how comfortable Dean moved in his skin. He angled and posed his body like a dancer.

"So pretty," Dean murmured one last time before turning to the business at hand: to probe without seeming to and to glean answers without asking a single question.

"So, Father Brocard," Dean began as he turned his chair around backwards and straddled it, "is a man damned if he sleeps with another man? That's what Leviticus says, right?"

"Judgment is God's alone," the priest replied. He thought it best to take the high road: The devil quotes Scripture just quote it back.

"I guess what I'm asking is, Are you judging, Father?" At this, Andy the clerk shifted at his desk, presumably to get a better angle on the conversation. "Word is that you were here last night checking up on who was getting off with who. If you know what I mean."

Anyone who knew Brocard well would have perceived his annoyance. But his years in Rome had trained him to be politic at even the most difficult of times. There was no way he would tip his hand to a worm like Dean.

"I do not have to explain my comings and goings to you, Dean. Nor do I have to answer to any such low accusations. Please leave my office now."

Dean responded with a smirk. "Well, look who's getting upset."

"Now, Dean," Brocard countered, not raising his voice but making it clear he was not playing around, "I will write you up if you don't get out now. And stay out."

Dean rose slowly, turned the chair around and moved toward the door. Then he pivoted slowly and said, in a tone so menacing that the memory of it stayed with Brocard for days, "Watch your step, little priest. You don't know what you're getting yourself into."

Before the priest could reply, Dean was gone.

Had Brocard truly stooped to playing puerile mind games with sadistic psychopaths? Surely there was a more professional way to deal with this. He knew he could write up a custody complaint and give Dean a charge: 60 days lockup, minimum, for threatening a staff member. But he knew if he did so, everything would be out in the open, especially his nocturnal investigations, which he knew he had to continue. He might have to turn over the photo he had found to some cretin in Internal Affairs. No, Dean knew what he was doing. He knew he needn't fear any retaliation from Brocard. He was not a dumb boy.

"You know, it's Dean who's distributing all of that anti-Catholic material," Andy offered, disrupting Brocard's musing.

"The Chick Tracts?" Brocard had nearly forgotten Andy was there, and quickly acknowledged the clerk's remark was a nod. He felt comforted that someone had witnessed the exchange with Dean. It was not the first time he had felt thankful for Andy's presence.

"Dean is caught up in that whole Officer Thomas thing," Andy continued. "Religion is just a gang activity for most people in here, Father. You should know that by now."

"I think Dean might be involved in a whole lot more than distributing blasphemous pamphlets," Brocard replied. He said no more, lest he give away too much.

But it was Andy, for reasons not easy to understand even now, who gave it away. "Drugs and liquor as well for sure. He's a runner, that Dean. A stupid runner. Nothing more."

Fourteen

THERE WAS NO QUIET CENTER TO BE FOUND, though he longed
for it mightily. How he could be expected, week after week, to
move from chaos into order was beyond him. Almost as a
reproach, he still heard the hopeful words of Father Matthias, his
novice master, reassuring him that at the very ground of his being
was a place of deep and abiding silence where God spoke to him.
It was to that place that a priest must go before celebrating the
Eucharist. It was on that quiet ground that he must stand to
escape the distractions of the world and the wiles of the devil.
How distant these words now seemed to Brocard.

From the moment he arrived at Brotherly Love on Sunday
mornings to set up for Mass, the priest was beset with problems. Some were systemic: It was simply daunting to move a
large group of inmates through the prison. But other challenges seemed to be obstacles set deliberately in his way, as if

some sinister force were conspiring to make him fail.

The keys themselves where enough to drive anyone to distraction. His chain, which he picked up at Center Control in exchange for a numbered voucher, had no fewer than 33 keys on it. Some remained a mystery to him. But he had to use at least half of them during the course of an average day. A large key let him into the long corridor that led to the chapel. Another key let him into his office. Next to his was a second office of equal size. Used only occasionally by the part-time chaplains for the Muslim, Protestant, and Jewish inmates, this office often sat undisturbed for days on end. It was littered with ancient memos and unopened mail.

This was not the case with Father Brocard's office, which he kept tidy as a pin. Every morning he had to unbolt the lock on his desk to take out and plug in his telephone, retrieve the keys for the two sturdy wooden cabinets where he stored all the materials for celebrating Mass, and unlock the small stationery closet next to Andy's desk. Paper clips and adhesive tape were dangerous contraband in prison. Brocard guarded his keys with his life.

This was just the start of the morning key saga. An especially large key opened the sliding doors that led into the chapel. Flicking on the half dozen wall switches, Brocard made his way down the stair and along the back wall of the chapel to the pair of old confessionals. Each booth was fitted with its own lock and each was put to a radically different use. The one on the right was now the J.C. Closet, prison-speak for Janitor's Closet. The cumbersome redundancy of the term always reminded Brocard how much spare time these boys had on their hands. Here, despite his frequent orders to do otherwise, his three porters often placed wet mops and garbage they were too lazy to take to the sally port (where everything coming into and going out of the institution was gathered). The old confessional to the left was used to store the statue of Our Lady of Guadalupe Brocard took out of hiding for Mass each week. The booth also lamentably held his vestments. The stomach-turning aromas from the J.C. Closet wafted freely into the vestment closet through the grill between them. There were times when Brocard shuttered to think of how he must have smelled as he reverenced the altar and began the sacred rites. Never an issue with most of the inmates (the Nose being a notable exception), for whom smell was the least-developed sense.

The morning key saga was far from over, although by the time Brocard reached the old confessionals, the telephone invariably started to ring, forcing him to run back to his office and interrupt his preliminary rounds. Usually, it was an officer calling to see whether a particular inmate, impatiently waiting at the gate, was cleared for a trip to chapel.

Returning to the back corner of the chapel after such a distraction, he unlocked the small gate that blocked access to the circular staircase leading up to the balcony. The balcony was undoubtedly the most misguided architectural feature of the entire chapel complex. Originally meant as a choir loft, it was now a favorite haunt of gangs and, Brocard sadly suspected, boys overcome with lust who needed some time alone. He made mental notes of the inmates who frequented the balcony during Mass. He came to doubt the piety of those who knelt behind the ranks of standing worshipers, or who jerked spasmodically while others were still.

From the stairs to the balcony he made his way to the front of the chapel, fumbling all the while with his keys. To the right of the sanctuary was the door to the sacristy, where the altar on wheels and songbooks were stored. He always took particular care in this area, with its own series of light switches and, more significantly, where his red phone waited for calamity. Custody never let him forget how he had accidentally knocked into it on one of his first days at work; officers with guns drawn poured into the chapel. Part of him was comforted to know it was there. Another more naive part of his brain believed such devices had no place in God's house.

There were still three more keys to use before he could even think of calling the inmates to help him prepare for Mass. The first was an odd, worn little key that opened a cabinet door under a ledge in the center of the sanctuary. There the altar candles, solid brass shanks, and tabernacle were kept. After he placed the tabernacle on the shelf, he had to open it with yet another key. Like his predecessor he knew he had to reserve the Eucharist, particularly for hospital calls, occasionally for Last Rites. He was also mindful of the designs of satanists in the prison. On his very first Sunday he'd noticed inmates trying to smuggle hosts to their cells after Communion. He tried to thwart this ploy by insisting that communicants place the host reverently into their mouths while he watched them. He had to ensure that none of the Body of Christ was stolen from the tabernacle to be used in black masses. About this possibility he was not so naive.

The last key was often the most difficult to locate because there was so little light in the far left corner of the chapel. There, the key opened a narrow door that led to a concealed corridor behind the curved wall of the sacristy. Why such a hidden space was ever allowed was another mystery—as were the contents at the far end of the room, which Father Brocard had never quite gotten around to exploring thoroughly. He stored the music stands and stools just inside the door. There was a tall ladder there as well, presumably used to patch the perpetually leaking skylights or to replace burnt-out lightbulbs. He promised himself that someday he would get around to cleaning the secret chamber to discover what treasures it held. But not just yet.

Andy was already at his desk when Brocard got back to the office. Inmates were never to be in offices without staff or custody present. But in this, as in so many things, Andy, universally trusted, was an exception. He was already giving the porters orders to bring down the altar linens and to fill the water cruet. Brocard couldn't have been more grateful for the help, especially when he noticed Dean and his cohorts lurking outside the office. He had to keep his eyes on them.

Beto, one of the Dominicano porters, a man who usually moved at a rather glacial pace, seemed agitated. "*Padre. Un momentito, por favor.*"

Brocard followed Beto into the chapel and over to the circular staircase. Glancing around to make sure no one had followed them into the chapel, Beto pointed a stubby finger toward the balcony. "No good in Jesus' house," he said, then lowered his voice to a whisper, "Flick books. You know: pornography."

They mounted the steps to the balcony and there, behind the last pew, Beto retrieved what he had found. He seemed genuinely distressed that such material was there, of all places. As was Brocard. Much as he disdained it, he had reluctantly come to see that pornography was endemic to prison life. Even so, it had no place in this sanctuary.

It was one of those moments, unfortunately not as rare as he would have liked, when Father Brocard wondered what on earth he was doing with his life. Was there any hope for these men? Was his ministry in any way meaningful? Or was it just some sort of sick joke? He was harried by a host of doubts as inmates began to arrive for Mass. Soon Cuchifrito would be rehearsing his repertoire of absurd songs. Jesucito and his gang of misfits would strive to make a mockery of God's Word. And the phone would ring off the hook.

Everything changed in an instant. As he followed Beto down from the balcony, Brocard stopped to thumb through the flick books. Not out of prurient interest, though at first Brocard wondered what had compelled him to open them. He was as asexual as ever. It was as if a hand was guiding him and he could but follow.

At the end of a tawdry visual tale about a boy and his dog—details to be spared—was a meticulously written list of names and addresses. Who could have hidden it there? When Dean avoided his gaze as he made his way back into his office, Brocard felt that question might soon have an answer. He knew the list was as yet another clue in the rapidly unfolding scandal at Brotherly Love Pen.

His suspicions were confirmed when he closed the door to his office and took out the list to inspect at it as carefully as he could in the few moments he had to spare before the gathered prisoners became impatient. One name jumped out at him: Pepe Castellano. Was this the information he needed? And Posillipo and Credit Suisse, Bahnhofstrasse. Italy and Zurich paired yet again.

He took out his keys to lock the flick books and the mysterious list in his desk. Glancing up from his key chain, he was surprised to see that Andy was somewhat agitated. But taking stock of his own state of mind, his pounding heart, his shaking hands, and his growing excitement, Brocard couldn't be sure of his assessment.

"Did you have them call out for Mass yet?" Andy queried him. Andy sensed the priest's distraction and knew Brocard had to get back on point.

"Sex and religion, manipulation and power, slaves and masters," he said in a monotone. "Hard to get a handle on any of it in here, isn't it, Father?" Then, making his way to the looking glass, he peered at himself and smiled. "Hard to even know what you're looking at, isn't it?"

Fifteen

ZINKA HAD LEARNED THAT TRUE LUXURY, FOR ANY LARGE woman, was space in which to breathe. Nothing was be more damaging to the spirit than feeling that the world was constructed for tiny people alone. Nothing more vexing than squeezing into a narrow airplane seat with inadequate space for mounds of flesh that were, under differing circumstances, the very embodiment of voluptuousness. And Zinka just had to have a window. No discussion. She had to know that the wing lights were on, the landing gear was working properly, and the air through which she was flying was clear and not filled with imminent danger. Never one to shirk responsibility, she made it her practice to instruct the stewardess to alert the pilot of anything she saw amiss. In her view, it was her plane to fly as well.

It did not help that she was swathed in several layers of pashminas and scarves, all of them diaphanously thin, to be sure, but nevertheless cumbersome in aggregate. As she wedged her way into her diminutive seat, her only hope was that no one would even consider sitting next to her. The aisle seat would not bother her—since the removal of her male genitalia she had developed excellent bladder control. Strangely, no one ever mentioned that positive benefit of the procedure. But a passenger plopping down in the middle seat would constitute a major problem.

No sooner had she begun to organize her things—a girl always has to have the essentials close at hand—than an uncommonly attractive Italian man sauntered down the aisle and eyed the seat next to her with predatory intensity. Despite the heavy assault of pheromones, Zinka did not (truth be known, she *could* not) budge.

Though a glance at his stub confirmed his right to the window seat, the suave stranger deferred to Zinka's resolute gaze and beguiling smile and took the aisle seat instead. He was, in truth, extremely stressed, having just stepped off a catwalk where he had been made to wear some of the most cockamamy couture ever foisted on a status-obsessed and aesthetically deadened public. The fact that some madcap designer had risen to the apogee of fame by fashioning eveningwear from bolts of rubber only stoked the flames of his anger. In addition to the designer's backstage tirades and the chafing he'd suffered in places best left unmentioned, he'd had to contend with the relentless advances of the old queens who buzzed around him like a cloud of nelly gnats. All of them were certain—"Don't be coy with me, I know it's true"—that anyone who wore rubber like he wore rubber just had to be into water sports.

Zinka knew nothing of her traveling companion's inner turmoil as she assembled the stack of books she needed to peruse in flight and struggled to secure her seat belt. Truth was, she had no time to think about this oversexed stud, no matter how adorable he might be. Her attention was focused on her flight, her reunion with her precious little Brocard, and the task ahead: the recovery of a Caravaggio nativity.

This did not mean Zinka was unaware of the deicing of the wings and the double-checking of the luggage as a gang of burly men loaded it into the hold beneath her. For once, she simply left these concerns to the professionals. As the cabin doors shut and the engines whirred to life, she preemptively spread her materials across the vacant middle seat. She noticed that her companion had closed his eyes and turned his head slightly away from her. Very unconvincing—trying to behave as if she and her affairs were of little interest to him. Zinka knew otherwise.

The first of the materials she had to read was the police report of the robbery, a copy of which was included in the Interpol file that Emile Rosenberg had obtained for her. Although the *fons et origen* of her research, the report seemed too straightforward, too short on details, to provide any real leads. As the plane slowly taxied down the runway, her mind returned to Vecchio Palermo, to those teeming alleys near the port, the site of several decadent holidays during those transitional years when Milorad had not yet given way to Zinka. Another story.

Now, in her mind's eye she saw the small Oratory of San Lorenzo, with its crumbling facade and bolted door. It had always been locked when she was there. Rarely was it used for prayer anymore, as there were far more impressive churches and basilicas in Palermo, each with its own weeping statues and miraculous relics. San Lorenzo had only one painting of note, a rather conventional early-17th-century nativity. And, even though it was uncontestedly by Caravaggio, despite the perfunctory grumbling of some experts, tourists and art historians alike rarely bothered to visit it. Should they have wished access, they would have had to first locate and then to cajole the unwelcoming Gelfollo sisters, controllers of the keys to the Oratory of San Lorenzo, which loomed just yards from their house on the other side of a dark alley. They alone could unlock the main door, they alone could put on the lights, and they alone could point out the cherubs capering on the wall that ran toward the alcove where the painting hung.

The morning of October 19, 1969, was gray and cheerless. When Maria, the elder of the two sisters, went out, she noticed a cat scampering through the open door of the Oratory. Although this was somewhat unusual, she was not alarmed. The place was crawling with cats. All of Palermo was, for that matter. Perhaps her sister, Amelia, who often rose earlier than she, had opened the chapel to do some cleaning. But on second thought, that didn't seem like something Amelia would do. Perhaps a tourist was trespassing. She began to worry.

What caught her eye first was the light on the elaborate runnel that traced the left side of the chapel under a row of windows. Never before had she noticed the sinuous sculpted lines directing the phalanx of cherubs on their riotous way to the Christ Child. Then she realized why. For the first time in her memory the window above the street was open. In fact, this was the first time she could remember seeing *any* window open. As any Sicilian knew, plague and disaster were carried by the wind. So long had these windows been sealed against the world, that no bars had ever been placed on them. As the sun flooded the runnels, Maria ran toward her nativity, the Caravaggio she had cherished and protected since she was a child, hoping against hope that her worst fears would not be realized. The tears came as quickly as her scream. *"Amelia! Vieni qui! Amelia!"* Grief wracked her body. Fragments of the painting she had loved as dearly as her life clung to the ornate frame. Those *bastardi* had hacked away at it and ripped it from where it had hung, undisturbed and tranquil, for over three and a half centuries.

When Amelia finally arrived, she began to wail, too. Two Sicilian mothers grieved the loss of their precious child—and berated themselves for imagined carelessness. Should the door have been bolted from the inside as well? It was so easy to unlock—perhaps a double lock would have helped. But how could the thieves have gotten away with the painting, which was nearly eight feet by seven feet, without attracting the attention of the neighbors? As anyone knows, the dark alleys of Vecchio Palermo have open eyes at any hour. Nothing goes unseen; no one goes unnoticed. Which was precisely the point at which the investigation started.

"Ladies and gentlemen, *mesdames et messieurs,* the captain has turned off the seat-belt sign." How had the plane taken off and reach cruising altitude without Zinka's attention? How could she have been so irresponsible? And where were the cocktails? Putting aside the riveting story of the disappearance of the Caravaggio nativity, she realized that her seat belt had tugged at her décolleté and pulled open the buttons on her blouse so that one breast, the one nearest her suddenly horny companion, was all but hanging loose. His face was aglow with the anticipatory look an infant saves for his wet nurse. As it happened, his deepest fantasy was to be trussed up in diapers while he sucked on a prodigious teat.

Zinka, eager to please, freed her breast completely from her blouse. *Time and money well spent,* she thought when she saw her companion's appreciative reaction to her carefully crafted *poitrine.* For the sake of decorum, she kept a scarf at hand, opaque enough to be discrete yet sheer enough not to frustrate a worshipful gaze.

As her companion played with himself under his blanket, Zinka wondered whether she should lead him to a lavatory to become better acquainted. However, she recalled the awkward if not embarrassing moment she'd endured on a previous flight during another amorous adventure. The facilities on board had proved inadequate to accommodate the statuesque Zinka and her slavering admirer. In fact, they'd not even managed to close the door. Earthy soul that she was, Zinka could not fathom why anyone would design such rooms for just one person. Toilets were meant to be shared: What fun is taking a good pee alone? Camille, prudish thing, could never quite get into this fetish and attributed it to Zinka's still thinking like a man. In any event, Zinka concluded she'd have to forego another *rendez-vous à la toilette.* This little chickie, hot and needy as he was, would have to handle his problem by himself.

For over an hour Zinka lost herself in another Interpol file. This one concerned a noble Inspector Siviero whose dangerous and admirable efforts to break the Mafia's hold on stolen art may well have precipitated the theft of the Caravaggio nativity. Although the evidence was circumstantial, it seemed conclusive. Retaliation for Siviero's successful case against a few front men may well have been the motive. And one name appeared in both the Interpol files and the list Brocard had recently E-mailed her: Pepe Castellano.

"Yes!" she exclaimed, throwing down the papers and exposing her proud, heaving bosom.

"Yes, yes," her companion said lurching in his chair. "Yes!"

Sixteen

THERE WAS NOTHING HE HATED MORE THAN FLOWING blood, especially his own. Once again he had caught the same old spot under his nose which, when he was stressed and anxious, he invariably cut when shaving. A styptic pencil would have done the trick, but, stupidly, Brocard could not remember the English word for it. A quarter of a century in Rome had depleted his vocabulary in his native language. And, having picked up some of the worst quirks of his adopted culture, he found it too much of a *brutta figura,* an insufferable embarrassment, to describe his disfigurement and to fumble for words in a pharmacy. No, when he knew what he had to ask for he would do it. Until then, he would suffer.

Compounding his problem was the blistering cold that forced him to wipe his nose periodically, thereby inevitably reopening his wound. For reasons he couldn't fathom, the entire chapel area and especially his office were as brutally cold as the wintry farm-lands outside. "Circuit-breaker problem or one of the feeder pipes" was all he could get out of anyone. When he had first arrived, he had seen Cavallo and one of the civilian staff members running around with blueprints. But as to where they were now and what on earth they were up to, he hadn't a clue.

Of course, he could not blame Zinka, even though it had been her arrival at Philadelphia International Airport that afternoon that had distracted him from his razor. No, the whole place was begin-ning to get to him: the craziness, the obfuscation, and the uncer-tainty. Was he deluding himself? These thoughts crowded his mind as he peered into the looking glass to examine the glistening dot of blood under his nostril. His excitable nature and unmitigated des-peration were turning a nick an absolute bloodbath.

"They're setting me up, Father Brocard," said Chopper, an extremely large, shockingly white inmate with a shaved head who had pushed his way into the office unannounced. Had they no social skills at all? "That's one nasty slash, Father. Who cut you up?"

"I did it to myself." Brocard replied as he tried valiantly to stanch the flow.

"Kinky," the inmate said with a leer. Before Brocard could explain that it was a shaving mishap, Chopper made himself at home and began his tale. "Here's what they're trying to pin on me."

"Who is trying to pin what on you, Chopper? Some facts first, please, before the dramatic narrative." Brocard folded up a fresh piece of toilet paper and pressed it firmly over his cut. Then he sat down at his desk and settled in for the long haul. "Facts, Chopper."

"That black officer on my house—you know the one. He's setting me up."

"That rather mousy-looking fellow who confiscated your white separatist material last month? Don't you think he might have some reason to hold a grudge, Chopper?"

"That was religious material—the Church of the Lily from God's Holy Mountain in Idaho. My lawyer is going to sue the hell out of this place for violating my rights."

"There is no right to hate, Chopper. Never was and hopefully never will be."

"It's not hate, Father Brocard. I'm a Christian." Try as he might—and he did his best approximation of a beatific smile—Chopper simply could not appear sympathetic. "Anyway, that's not the problem. It's when I was conversating with Wolfy."

"Poor Wolfy, are they still overmedicating him? Last time he came to chapel, he looked like a zombie." Brocard was so glad medications were Doctor Pouri's call. Personally, he thought it cruel to numb inmates into innocuous dysfunction. He believed that healing and change more readily occurred when the confusion and anxiety weren't swept under the rug.

"Him and me have a really good rapport," Chopper averred.

Although bad grammar insulted his very being, Brocard had trained himself not to correct inmates while they were conversating—conversing, that is.

"What was it that you were talking about then?" Brocard probed.

"Nothing much. About how you got to jail in here, you know what I'm saying?" Presuming Father Brocard understood his prison patois, Chopper continued. "This is a sweet bit, you know what I'm saying, if you jail it?"

Brocard was familiar with the way inmates learned the system: Whom to know to get what, where to go to get by. Prison was as much a school of crime as a place of punishment. When he first arrived, the priest had hoped that being locked up would teach inmates right from wrong. The sad reality, he quickly learned, was that Brotherly Love was a way of life for most of the souls who passed through its door.

"So Wolfy gives me his meds, you know, because they lied on him."

"Who lied to him, Chopper?"

"Some new dude. Worth nothing. Anyway Wolfy can just sit on this dude to shut him up. So when the altercation had took place…"

"Let me get this straight." Brocard interrupted. He strained to bring logic to the situation, though he was not convinced it would move them any nearer the truth. "You told Wolfy to stand up for himself, and you held his medications for him while he went off to pummel some dude who was hitting up on him?"

Brocard couldn't believe he had actually spoken these words. Was he so far gone?

"Yeah, that's it, Father," Chopper replied, obviously impressed. "You're not too bad at jailing yourself."

"I am not saying I agree with any of this, Chopper. I am just trying to figure out how I can help you, that's all."

"So you know this zero-tolerance thing, right? If you have another person's meds on you, it's like the same as having drugs."

Brocard nodded. "And the officer who you believe has it in for you presumably saw Wolfy handing his medications to you and moved in on you. Charging you with possession, I presume?"

"I'm not beat, Father. You know what I mean. I'm not beat."

Fortunately, just when Chopper might reasonably have expected Brocard to offer some wisdom or, worse still, positive intervention, Andy returned to the office. He had been out delivering the memos announcing Dr. Zinka Pavlic's arrival at Brotherly Love the next day. In the memo Brocard assured all concerned that she had been duly cleared by Internal Affairs and that she would be leading a new behavior-modification class as a fully approved volunteer.

"Andy, good thing you're here. We have work to do," Brocard said hastily. Then, looking steadily at Chopper, he explained he might not be able to do very much. He arranged a meeting with Wolfy to hear his side of the story and then with the officer to learn whether he had indeed written up the incident up. Perhaps the whole affair would amount to nothing. But now—*sorry*—he had other things to do. He promised Chopper he'd do his utmost and encouraged him to check in later.

Although Chopper found it hard to believe that anything could be more pressing than his own affairs, he reluctantly agreed to let things be for the moment. "So it's going to take like a bit of time. All right then, for now," he said in parting.

Andy closed the door behind Chopper as he left. He obviously had something to tell Brocard and he needed to make sure no one disturbed their conversation.

"You have to call Jesucito down now," Andy said, his eyes wide. "I'll explain while he's coming." As Brocard pulled the directory from his drawer and dialed the appropriate housing officer, Andy looked at Brocard with a perplexed expression. "Father, I hope you won't mind my asking. Why do you have a piece of toilet paper hanging out of your left nostril?"

"I cut myself shaving." Brocard replied. He spoke these words into the receiver, whereupon he had to thank the officer for his concern and assure him that the chaplain had not called the housing unit only to inform them that he had brutalized himself with a razor. "Thank you anyway," Brocard said to the baffled officer, "But could you please just send inmate Jesucito to my office."

It was time for Brocard to take the toilet paper off his lip and get on with his life. Making his way to the mirror, he gently removed the bloodstained wad and tried not to disturb the scab. He was almost successful.

"Just a little bit of blood still," he said. "It seems to be coagulating well."

"If you don't mind my prying," Andy said, as eager for blood as any bat. "How many hours have you been trying to get it to stop?"

"On and off for about two hours, I guess. Not bad as these things go."

"Great for a hemophiliac to be sure," Andy replied. "Ever had this checked into?" Brocard saw no reason for Andy's alarm. Sooner or later the bleeding always stopped." You might have a vitamin K deficiency," Andy speculated. "No big deal, but you should have it looked into."

"I must say I have never heard of vitamin K." Brocard's tone made it clear he would be quite happy to drop the topic completely. But Andy, displaying the tenacity of a dog with a bone, had no desire to let things lie.

"It's something of a rich-bitch deficiency, if you'll excuse me saying so, Father. Anorexic and bulimic girls get it a lot. Rarer in guys, but I guess you're neither one nor the other, are you?" Brocard was not insulted as he heard Andy's remark, as he saw it as a commendation of his celibacy rather than as the facetious slur Andy had intended. "You can take a supplement for it. Lots of people I used to know in my past life took them. Beats eating organ meats and kale, which I believe are major food sources."

"Shouldn't we talk about why we've called down Jesucito?" he asked in exasperation. Andy finally got the point and mercifully moved on.

"You just have to see what's up with Jesucito," Andy replied cryptically. There was a playful lilt in his voice that caused Brocard to hope in vain for a festive reprieve from the insanity around him. "He's self-mutilating again. The balls I think. Anyway, you'll see, he can't hide the blood."

No, this was not the break Brocard had in mind. A quirky little conversation would have done nicely, or even a mild psychotic break. But not this.

Just then Jesucito appeared at the door, his shoulders slumped and head hanging even lower than ever usual. He looked drained of all color—except the wet crimson patch that spread across the crotch of his trousers. Suddenly, Brocard's nick seemed a minor thing, and his facility with words failed him. Fortunately, it was Jesucito who initiated and in fact controlled the conversation. There were things he had to say.

"Meester Brocard," the inmate began. As with Officer Thomas, this was the form of address that, despite all his arguments to the contrary, Father Brocard had come to expect from Jesucito and several of his Fundamentalist disciples. "Call no one Father except my Father in heaven," Jesus had said. (Paul, nevertheless, had referred to himself as "Father.") Still, it was a minor issue, and what concerned Brocard now was how "devoid of affect," as his psychologist friends would put it, Jesucito had become. It was as if his life force had been drawn out of him, leaving behind nothing recognizable—that is, until he spoke.

"Meester Brocard, she has come to me again," Jesucito continued.

Who, exactly? Brocard's gaze inquired.

"The seester of the daimon."

"The devil's sister?" Brocard asked. Andy pulled his chair

nearer the door where Jesucito stood, blood dripping from his crotch. "Which one?"

"The beeg sister." Brocard was too confused to notice that Andy appeared to understand what this poor delusional young man was saying. Worse still, he seemed to be goading Jesucito on. "She come in my *cojones* and I have to crush her out with de Bible. And cut her out if she stay."

"Crushing and cutting his balls, Father," Andy interjected. "Sounds like a case for Doctor Pouri, I think."

"The daimon tell me he is here in de chapel," Jesucito continued. "The daimon he not crazy." At this Jesucito raised his head and looked first at Brocard then at Andy and then looked down.

"Jesucito," Brocard replied, "I am going to try to help you get rid of the demons. You must believe me, I want to help." Then, going over to the boy, Brocard placed his hand on Jesucito's shoulder and assured him that nothing bad would happen to him. "We'll get you help, that's all."

Brocard asked Andy to follow Jesucito back to his cell and to tell his housing officer to keep an eye on him until someone from Psychology arrived. Then he left a message on Dr. Pouri's answering machine to explain what had happened. He hoped that, at the very least, Jesucito would be moved to the Ad Seg Unit while he was under observation. Brocard did not realize this would put Jesucito in Officer Thomas's clutches, a situation that would only feed the inmate's neurosis. At that moment, Brocard's only thought was get to the airport to pick up his wonderful old friend, whose craziness, he hoped, was bound to get his mind off the madness that was Brotherly Love.

Seventeen

"YES, THIS WILL DO ME JUST FINE," Zinka purred. "Now don't worry your little head about the rather cramped space and funereal drapes or the tawdry antiques. What more does a girl need, anyway? It will be just fine for me."

Brocard wanted so much for things to be right. Not just because his was a classic pleaser-personality, but because this was, remarkably, his friend Zinka's first trip to the States. For once he displayed a typically American trait: an obsession with making his guest feel welcome.

"Mrs. O'Connor, the housekeeper, is looking forward to meeting you when she comes in tomorrow," Brocard prattled nervously. "She assured me that this is the warmest guest room in the rectory. Unfortunately, it hasn't been redone in years, as you can see. It's clean, though. Mrs. O'Connor sees to that. The pastor isn't too big on visitors, but that's a whole other story. The main problem I see is that your room doesn't have its own bathroom. Monsignor Duhmbelle's suite just down the hall on the right has the only attached bath. I use the small one across from his, just over there to the left of the hall. It's big enough for both of us."

"Sharing a toilet," Zinka mused. "How *intime*. What a precious, absolutely precious idea." That was not what Brocard had in mind, of course. And Zinka knew better than to read salacious intent into the priest's arrangements. But she did so love to get her bald cleric friend going. So she squelched his protestations by kissing her finger, sealing it over his lips, and giggling in the most delightfully demure way. Let no one tell you that coming to womanhood in middle age is a simple affair, for guile is not easy to learn.

In fact, Zinka was perfectly satisfied with her lodgings. On the ride from Philadelphia International Airport she braced herself for the worst. It did not help that Brocard, whose sense of direction was notoriously bad, got hopelessly lost on his way out to the Main Line. After an interminable wander through dark and forbidding streets with no aesthetic merit whatsoever, it was a positive relief to arrive in Bryn Mawr, where solid piles kept a respectful distance from one another. Even the teetering mounds of shoveled snow looked architecturally distinguished in moonlight.

Zinka was particularly impressed by Our Lady of Perpetual Help. Such a sturdy building it was, with a fine oak staircase perfect for grand entrances and a turreted window with a *banquette* where a lady might sit of an evening, thumbing carelessly through a book of poetry, her hair tumbling down her back. Yes, Zinka knew she would be quite comfortable in her new environment.

Next to staying in a monastery, which she had not yet managed, spending time in a rectory was her fondest dream. The reason was obvious: The very notion of celibacy was so alien to her that she tingled with excitement even to think of such a place. The search for transcendent peace and the practice of piety held no charms for her. No, not for Zinka. Rather, it was the sheer volume of suppressed anxiety and the imminent explosion of testosterone that filled her with eager expectation.

"Now, Father," she said. "Unless you are intent on following me to the toilet, I suggest you go to the kitchen and make us a pot of tea. Let me unpack a few frocks. I'll just freshen up a bit and gather together my Caravaggio notes and join you in a few minutes."

After making sure Zinka had all the towels she needed and knew how to close the curtains—she had already begun to unbutton her blouse—Brocard obediently left the room. As he left he remembered he had neglected to tell her where the kitchen was. But as they are always in the rear of old houses, he correctly presumed she would find her way.

As excited as Father Brocard was about Zinka's arrival and as comfortable as he was with her minor eccentricities, he could not help feeling he should have been more thorough in the description he'd given the pastor in whose rectory he was lived. Monsignor Duhmbelle was not a very sociable creature. In fact, he was both an introvert and a misanthrope, which made living with him a daily trial. Between Brocard and Duhmbelle there was no communication worth speaking of. Not that Brocard was that needy—he was at heart still a monk and the occasional grunt or raised eyebrow provided all the human contact he required. But Duhmbelle skulked around to avoid Brocard at every juncture. When Brocard was to say Mass, he learned of his assignment from a note Duhmbelle left on his place mat.

Brocard had spoken about Zinka to Mrs. O'Connor, who was as garrulous as the pastor was taciturn. "All the way from Paris, don't you know?" she exclaimed in her rich brogue. "Now isn't that something to think about? No, it won't do to tell the Monsignor about her being a woman." Brocard had wanted to interject that Zinka hadn't always been a woman. Perhaps not clarifying her sex got closer to the truth than specifying it boldly. But Mrs. O'Connor's questions were never meant to be answered. Nor, for that matter, would it have been easy to squeeze a word in, as the questions tumbled one on top of another in seemingly endless succession. "You mentioned she was a doctor? Not, don't you know, a doctor you can do much with, I guess? Like most of those doctors over there at the College, isn't she? Not much help if anything is ailing you, are they?

Worried that the truth might prompt Duhmbelle to decline the visit, Brocard decided to write a note that contained most of the truth, just not all of it: "I have extended an invitation to stay to Dr. Pavlic, a distinguished art historian with ties to Bryn Mawr and an old friend of mine from Paris."

The note he received in reply was equally terse. "Mrs. O'Connor will find a room for Dr. Pavlic at some distance from ours. Let this be the last time you ask for such a privilege."

Tea was one of the few things Brocard could pull off in a kitchen with any assurance. He knew how to pour boiling water into the pot, how to measure the proper amount of loose tea, and how long to steep it so that it would not become overly acidic. Of course, the timing depended on Zinka's coming down in the near future. In fact, she had long ago readied herself but, snoop that she was, she had decided to take a house tour before joining her friend for tea. Jet lag did nothing to dampen her curiosity.

Brocard's room, across the hall from hers, was totally predictable. So spare and plain and uninviting. So monkish. It was obvious that the oversized furniture and superfluous throw rugs stuffed into every other room had been evicted from his chamber and stored in the attic for the duration of his stay. His bathroom, too, was devoid of everything except the barest necessities. Not a single bottle of cologne, not even a loofah. Nothing but toothpaste and soap. Chilling.

Now the pastor's room was worth lingering over. A bit overdone perhaps—plenty of extra throw-cushions on the king-size bed and chintz balloon valances on the Liberty-curtained windows—but Zinka could handle indulgence far better than asceticism. What amused her to no end was his vanity table. Yes, even though it was most likely an antique that came with the house, the Monsignor had curiously chosen to keep and use a woman's vanity. On it were the most elaborate brushes, with handles of pressed silver and mother-of-pearl, lined up as if for some ritual combing. She longed to sit down and lose herself in the mirror, like the baroque Magdalen she pictured herself to be. But even Zinka knew that discretion was in order. And, anyway, tea would surely be ready.

"Well, what do you think?" she asked as she twirled into the kitchen with her arms wide open to reveal the pleats and elaborate patterning of a kimono robe—part of the seemingly endless inheritance from Camille's clotheshorse of a mother.

"And you are?" a stern voice queried in reply.

She had spun straight into the face of Monsignor Duhmbelle, more sour-faced than ever and more than a little perplexed. "I might ask the same of you," she parried.

Brocard had been so busy finding the cups and laying them out that he had not noticed either of them enter until it was too late. Still, no better time than the present to make the necessary introductions.

"Monsignor Duhmbelle, this is my friend Dr. Zinka Pavlic. Zinka, Monsignor Duhmbelle."

Trying to control himself, the Monsignor could only say, "I thought you were a man."

"That problem has plagued me my whole life, darling," Zinka replied. "You're not the first."

"Dr. Pavlic just got in from Paris, Monsignor," Brocard hastily added. Strange how Brocard, who was on first name basis with provincial generals and bishops, could never bring himself to call Duhmbelle by his first name. Nor would such familiarity have been welcome if he did. "We were just going to have a cup of tea. Would you care to join us?"

Looking at Brocard in disbelief, Monsignor Duhmbelle excused himself to Zinka and asked to see Brocard in the next room. Out of earshot, he laid into the hapless monk.

"How dare you bring a woman into this house," he hissed. "Do you know nothing about canon law? About giving scandal? And such a woman. Loose and, well, full-figured at that."

This was the most Brocard had ever heard the pastor speak. Though he knew—or at least Mrs. O'Connor had told him—that the good Monsignor had another house furnished with a live-in mistress, Brocard didn't quite know what to say. Perhaps he had not been totally honest about Zinka's gender, but the simple truth was that she was a friend and a good one at that. Nothing more to it. No hypocrisy on his end to worry about, at least. And no reason to back down.

"Dr. Pavlic is here to do research," he said, an edge of boldness in his voice. "She will be staying for the amount of time she needs. After she leaves I will apply to the bishop for other lodgings in the diocese. You will be troubled with me no longer."

Duhmbelle was speechless. He had just found out what many before him had learned. Although small and seemingly compliant, Father Brocard was not to be trifled with—especially when he knew, as he surely did now, that he was in the right.

When Brocard returned to the kitchen, Zinka had already poured the tea and was fastening her hair in a chignon, something Camille had only recently taught her. It was not the most flattering of looks on her, as her jaw had a Joan Sutherland (or was it Nick Nolte?) cut to it. Still, she had a beguiling smile that softened everything.

"Now just you calm down," she soothed. "Have tea and forget about that strange little man."

"He is the pastor," Brocard said glumly. "After all, it is his rectory."

"And his vanity table," Zinka said, her eyebrows arched. She took a sip of tea and told Brocard all about her little snoop. "No wonder his hair has fallen out—he has probably pulled it out because of some obsessive-compulsive disorder. *Elle* had a whole article on it recently. And the way he torments those few long strands above his ear into a thin web is positively creepy. Don't give him another thought, my dear little Brocard. Now, it's time to get to work."

Eighteen

HE HAD PRACTICED ALL THE TECHNIQUES, and even taught
them: how to breathe and clear the mind. How to open oneself
up to God waiting within. He had all the tools of a contempla-
tive and bore all the hallmarks of a spiritual adept. But for the
life of him, Brocard could not quiet his mind. After all that had
happened the night before, after the collision of two entirely
different yet fully comprehensible worlds—Zinka's and the pastor's—everything was noise and confusion. He resigned himself
to not finding that still center—the ground of his being, as they
called it in the monastery—which so refreshed him at the
beginning of each day. Sadly, the more he longed for it, the more
elusive it became. Still, he was covetous of his hour of medita-
tion and Mass. Always—no matter how little he had slept, nor
how difficult it was to think of higher things—he thanked God
for that time, as he sat in the chapel, appearing to everyone but

his God like a man fully at peace and deep in prayer.

However, here in the kitchen, concentrating on drawing in his breath, Zinka in all her frenzied glory was all that he could see. And as he exhaled slowly into the world, the words of the Jesus Prayer, his mantra of choice, were inaudible over the recollected din of her delightful diatribe.

"See here what I have found," she had said excitedly. She cleared away the teapot and moved the napkin holder to place a pile of papers in front of him. "These are copies of the lists of names and addresses kept by the three suspects in the *Palermo Caravaggio* heist." Zinka was clearly pleased with herself for using the word "heist," and explained rather sheepishly that she had heard it on *The Sopranos,* her very favorite program.

Brocard pored over the photocopies of hastily scribbled notations, trying to share Zinka's enthusiasm but, for the life of him, he couldn't decipher anything in front of him.

"You are so adorable when you pretend to be dense," Zinka purred. Moving her chair nearer his and rearranging the papers into three neat piles, she explained matters in a tone better suited to a class for the learning disabled. "First, remember what I E-mailed you about Inspector Siviero? The brave, if not foolhardy, investigator who decided that he would bring down the Mafia single-handed? Everything started with the *heist*—how I love that word—of a lovely statue known as an ephebus, a bronze dating from the fifth century before Christ. A unique piece, the only known example of pre-Greek Sicilian workmanship. Worth millions now and well over a million even 33 years ago when it was stolen. Are you with me, dear?"

"*Sì, Professoressa.*" Brocard quite enjoyed being condescended to by an effete pedant. They were so hard to find in jail. And Zinka was so obviously enjoying herself.

"After an elaborate sting operation," she continued, "three suspects, all minor Mafiosi, were nabbed red-handed with the ephebus." At this linguistic feat, Brocard could not help but gasp.

"Good God, Zinka! 'Sting,' 'Mafiosi,' 'nabbed,' and 'red-handed'!

Do you live for *The Sopranos*? Or does colloquial gang-talk just come naturally to you?"

"Now you're starting to sound like Camille," Zinka chided. But she could not suppress a smile. "Well, perhaps I do tape a program or two and replay them when I'm doing my toilette. Such an exotic, delicious tale." Then, catching herself, she returned to the subject at hand.

"Now listen, silly. Less than a week after these three convicted robbers were released from prison—after having spent a pathetic few months there, thanks to the total incompetence and corruption of the Italian courts—our *Caravaggio* was stolen from San Lorenzo. Eyewitness accounts never verified these suspicions because, of course, no one would step forth. But considerable circumstantial evidence led Inspector Siviero to believe that these same three culprits were responsible. At first the motive seemed to be no more than revenge. You know, 'I'll show you what the fuck—'"

Brocard stopped her. "Not here Zinka, please. I don't approve of such language. We're in a rectory, remember. Anyway, I get your point."

She regarded him affectionately. "You are such a little prude, aren't you?" Then, pulling her chair unduly close to his and invading his personal space, she sighed, "If only we weren't so busy solving crimes."

"But we are, Zinka," he replied, shifting his chair over a bit. At this rate, they would be making a full turn of the table in under an hour. "There is a crime to solve."

Father Brocard could only smile as he considered her irreverence. He was, after all, trying to meditate before Mass, trying to still his mind, though the memory of Zinka's manic presence would not let him be. But perhaps on some level his mind was still. He began to realize all of last night's silliness had a purpose. Weren't all the pieces falling into place? He could make out the shuffle of the altar servers as they passed in front of him to light the candles for Mass and the rustle of missalettes as the daily communicants gathered in the front pews to prepare for Mass. The thought that they might be interpreting his Zinka-induced smirk as a beatific vision nearly broke him up. But he would not be deterred. There was time still before he had to celebrate the sacrament. Time to replay the conversation of the night before and to allow all of its revelations to tumble recklessly in his mind.

Zinka took the files from Brocard and sifted though them. "These lists, you see, are photocopies of names and addresses found in the apartments or cars of the three suspects. By comparing them, it's clear," here she spread them out and indicated corresponding scribbles, "that they all point to one man, Don Pepe Castellano, by all reports one of the kingpins of the operations that extend from drugs to fine art and everything in between."

With a flourish Brocard took two lists of his own out of his pocket and unfolded them on the table. The first was the one found in Tony Polluto's cell after his apparent suicide. In a low voice, worried that the pastor might still be within earshot, he read it out loud: "'Heroin from Burma Buddha to Pennsy Amish; Crack from PR Santería to Harlem Five-Percenters; Cigarettes from Bible Belt to Bible City; Caravaggio from Sicilian Catholics to Zurich Zwinglis.'" Then, looking at Zinka, he said, "All the goodies a boss like Castellano might be able to get his hands on?"

"Precisely," Zinka agreed. Then, almost as a caution, she said, "But remember, my dearest little Brocard, we are here to break the Caravaggio mystery. Drugs have nothing to do with us."

"Don't worry," Brocard replied. "If my suspicions are right, they will take care of themselves. Solving the one will lead the way to the other. God willing, we will not have to soil our hands." In fact, his hands began to tremble slightly as he opened the second piece of paper—the one he had found in the choir loft of the chapel. Clearing his throat, he read it to her.

"'Don Pepe, Vico Equense, CAPO123@solutions-inc.com.'" Then, hastily trying to explain away the page of scribbles in front of him, "there is more here, of course, but this is surely what we need, don't you think? Corroboration of your lists? Lead information that will take us to where we need to go?"

"Perhaps," Zinka said cryptically. "We have only one way of finding out, my dear." Rising imperiously from the table and pressing the creases out of her dressing gown, she signaled like a scout indicating the safe passage between enemy lines. "To the computer!" As they scampered upstairs like children on an Easter egg hunt—or so it seemed to Brocard, as he played the scene over in his mind—he felt a tug at the sleeve of his alb.

"Father. Father. Excuse me, Father, but it is time for Mass." He opened his eyes to see Megan, his favorite altar server: punked-out hair, black lacquered fingernails, and the most earnest of looks. God bless her, she had set up everything. Cruets on the credence table, chalice and paten in place, and sacramentary opened to the introit. So modern, yet so beguilingly traditional. A girl after his own heart.

As he put on his stole and chasuble, those last minutes with Zinka at the computer lingered in his mind. Camille, she felt, would love to have a task. What better assignment for her than contacting Interpol at her end to find out what she could about Don Pepe Castellano? What about this link with Vico Equense, that lovely little resort town just north of Sorrento? Was the Don a suspect in other art thefts? Could he even be reached or, like so many people at the top, was he insulated from everything and everyone?

Brocard smiled as he made his way to the altar, reverenced it, and made the sign of the cross. "The Lord Be with You," he intoned. And as he received the formal greetings of the congregation he considered how excited Zinka was to be able to include Camille in this adventure. *How curious human relationships are,* he thought. *How inscrutable and beautiful.*

As the ritual of the Mass took over, Brocard's body began to relax. All the mania that had been swirling around him vanished. With candles burning and bells signaling the elevation of the host, he found that center he had almost feared lost. And, knowing it might not last for long, held on to it tenaciously.

Nineteen

"TIGHTER. TIGHTER. STRETCH THEM OUT. Pull them tighter until you can't bear it," Zinka commanded.

From what she gathered, this was the proper way to conduct the pre-class meditations prescribed in the behavior-modification manual. In a seated position, with eyes closed, her students extended their arms and legs as far as they could, literally pulling out all the stress and relaxing all the muscles. Of course, they were supposed to be on chairs and not on the floor, and the female instructor was not supposed to be wearing a skirt so short that it rode up to her panties and a blouse so décolleté that her breasts threatened to pop out. The vision that was Zinka made it difficult for most of the inmates in the class—those whose libidos were still intact—to keep their eyes shut for long or to even begin to picture the calm scene the manual described. None of this fazed Professoressa Zinka Pavlic as she stretched and twisted her voluptuous form before the inmates' eager eyes.

"Hands up, I said, Mr. Cavallo'" Zinka chided. "No need to scratch down there right now, and no peeking. This is the time to picture your calm scene. Remember how we talked about having a calm scene? Breathe deep and stretch and tighten and put yourself right where you want to be."

Zinka couldn't guess that Cavallo was not the inmate's real name. But she would have been amused to know why he had been given it. If she were not so intent on being a good teacher— or at least intent on not blowing her cover—she would have noticed the massive erection growing before her. She inspired several in fact, though none, of course, as prodigious as that of Mr. Horse. Other things, however, were becoming clear to her. The quest for clarity was, after all, why she was there: to learn more about the list of suspects. To discover the hand behind the chaos at Brotherly Love Pen. Ultimately, to recover the elusive Caravaggio *Holy Family* and restore it to its rightful place.

Brocard, God bless his compulsive little heart, thought ceaselessly about their investigation. He had narrowed the list of possible suspects to a handful. But he also knew himself well enough to realize he needed an objective eye, someone not so immersed in these inmates' lives, to see the bigger picture. He had contrived to have all his suspects enroll in the new volunteer program so that she might see them for who they really were.

Lest the cunning culprits catch on to his scheme, Brocard played on their universal fatal flaw: vanity. Participants in Zinka's class thought they had been chosen because they were the best and the brightest (or the most incorrigible). As long as he made them feel special, Brocard could get away with almost anything.

Zinka suddenly realized she had conflated two parts of the relaxation exercise. No wonder it wasn't working! First the stretching of the muscles, then relaxing, breathing, and entering the calm space. She mumbled *"merde"* a few times, which allowed her to regain her composure. Pretending she had done nothing wrong and that she was fully in command—doubly absurd illusions—she stood up and spoke to each inmate in turn.

As she moved around the room, she was thankful Brocard had taken the time to debrief her on the history of each inmate and that she was blessed with a good memory for names.

"Andy," she said, addressing the clerk. "You can drop your arms now and just picture your calm scene." Who was it Andy reminded her of? Why did he look so familiar? And where on earth did he get that air of superiority? You would have thought he was someone of importance.

"Conjure, Dean. Conjure it up." The surly prisoner regarded Zinka with undisguised contempt. "And close your eyes. Now." It was clear he had an attitude problem. Instinctively—and in this she was fully a woman—she knew he was up to no good. Perhaps he was the one.

"Jesucito. Jesucito, come in." Either the boy had gone into a catatonic state or he was assuredly dead. "I said, picture your calm space. No out-of-body experiences, please."

Jesucito slowly opened his eyes and lifted his hands, as if in prayer.

"Oh, good. I wouldn't want to lose one of you on day one," Zinka said with relief. Reconsidering, she added, "Or on any other day, for that matter." Then, bending over Jesucito, she said reassuringly, "Now you won't give *Professoressa* any more scares, will you?"

In truth, Jesucito wasn't scaring anyone. It was she who caused a fright! To him, she was all he desired—the devil's very sister—and her breasts hanging pendulously before him filled him with positively delicious fear.

Not the case with Cavallo, who rapturously inspected Zinka's rump as she conversed with Jesucito. Even at her most maternal, Zinka could arouse passion. In a happy coincidence, ass sex worked best for both Zinka and Cavallo. Since his incarceration, he had become accustomed to a sphincter—he even preferred its harsh, tight fit. And despite the success of her operation, Zinka wasn't entirely comfortable with her newly constructed vagina, and preferred instead the tried-and-true rear entry. In brief: Zinka and Cavallo were made for each other.

On some deep (or perhaps some remarkably superficial)

level, Zinka must have known this. When she caught sight of Cavallo inspecting her behind, she could not bear to remove it from his view, but rather allowed him to admire it as much as he liked. *These poor boys,* she thought, working her dress up a bit, *have so few pleasures.*

"Now, slowly feel the air caressing you," she instructed. "Remember, you are good and life is beautiful." She could not help feeling like the inane Roberto Benigni as she mouthed these words. In fact, she believed the manual was unadulterated crap. But she had been an academic for so long that her tolerance for rubbish was as high as her need for truth was low. In other words, she was able to play her new role without any pesky interference from her conscience. "Fill your mind with whatever your goal is. Fixate on it, my precious little felons, and breathe deep."

As the exercise ended, she cooed, "When I count to 10, you will open your eyes and return to this room, reluctantly leaving your calm scene behind." There was no difficulty there, to be sure. Between Jesucito's anxiety over the devil, Cavallo's hormones, Dean's unadulterated contempt, and Andy's attitude of noblesse oblige, these calm scenes, if they had ever existed at all, were already long gone. "Eight. And nine. And 10. Now open your eyes."

The final part of the class was taken up with a discussion topic. The options included self-esteem, about which Zinka knew much, and cognitive distortion, which, for the life of her, made no sense whatsoever. Because it seemed the easiest topic to tackle, especially in the first class, she chose assertiveness. *Surely inmates,* she foolishly thought, *will have no problem with this.*

"Assertiveness is not aggressiveness," she began. "Let me give you an example. Now, how is a woman like me supposed to deal with the injustices of organized religion toward those of my sex? Let's be more specific: As I am Roman Catholic and proud of it, how do you think we women should handle being locked out of the ministry? We, who look good in dresses, whom God had chosen to adorn with bright and festive colors, are not allowed to wear pink silk on Gaudate Sunday or teal on the Assumption? Does it make sense?"

At this Dean could control himself no longer. First, she'd asked him to conjure something up—a task more appropriate to black magic than to the chaplaincy, which sponsored this preposterous class. Now, she asked him to deny Scripture itself.

"First Corinthians 14, verse 34," he mumbled.

"What was that, Mr. Dean? Speak up so we can all hear."

"Not everyone here has to hear it," he sneered. "Only you. The Word of God says, 'Women should keep silent in the churches, for they are not allowed to speak.'"

Clearly taken aback but not willing to be derailed, Zinka forged on without answering his fundamentalist assault. "The point is, I can either scream and try to force my right to open participation in the church—that would be the aggressive way and that more often than not gets us nowhere—or I can assert my rights by being strong and reasonable."

"Whore!" spat Jesucito, coming back to life. Zinka instantly changed her mind about him. It would have been better, for her, at least, if he had remained catatonic. Running from the room, he screamed, "Whore of Babylon! Temptress of Sheba! Sister of the Daimon!"

Jesucito ran smack into Father Brocard, who watched in amazement as the entire class disintegrated into chaos. *Good old Zinka,* he thought. *She certainly has her ways.*

Twenty

INVISIBLE SHE WAS NOT. YET GIVEN THE right circumstances, enough distractions, and an uncharacteristic amount of self-control, Zinka made an excellent snoop. This she proved at the prison Mass the following weekend.

Her objective was simple: to see for herself whether there was any conspiratorial web and, if so, to find out who, if anyone, was its leader. From Brocard she learned that the chapel was the only unsupervised meeting place open to the entire institution. It was also the only area with neither surveillance cameras nor a regular stationed officer. If any gang meeting were to take place out of Custody's eye, this would surely be the place for it. However, Brocard dismissed the idea that these activities went on in the chapel. Perhaps sporadically, he allowed, but surely in no organized way. Zinka—familiar as she was with the best and worst in men—had her suspicions. And what better way to confirm this than to catch them red-handed?

She waited until after the service was underway—well after the readings from scripture had begun—to make move. During the tour of the chapel Brocard gave her, she had noticed a back door to the choir loft, or "playpen," as she had heard several inmates rather impiously refer to it. Fortunately, Sergeant Kraus was at Center Control—nothing like having a sister at hand when you need her—and Zinka had no problem persuading the stout Bavarian to unlock the door for her. In fact, from the steely look in the good sergeant's eyes, Zinka gathered she was willing to offer other services as well. But, as the sacrament called, Doctor Pavlic could only give Kraus one of her "I'm all yours next time" winks.

Once inside, Zinka stealthily made her way to the abandoned organ in the back of the loft and sat on the bench. There were only half a dozen inmates in the four rows of pews; most preferred to pack themselves in downstairs. Two inmates appeared to be negotiating some deal. One withheld a package from another, who stared at him angrily, as if the other man had gone back on a promise. The other four men knelt motionless in the front row.

While they had not noticed Zinka—a good thing—it was obvious to her that the balcony railing was blocking her view, which was definitely not helpful for her purpose. To see anything, she would have to move forward a few pews or, better still, get herself higher up so that she could see what was happening below. She realized that if she sat on top of the organ— not like some slut but ladylike, because this was God's house, after all—she would be able to take in the entire congregation below. There was a slight chance Brocard might see her. But since the old monk was nearsighted, she believed it was a chance worth taking. Anyway, he had invited her to come to Brotherly Love Pen to do some sleuthing!

The sight of Zinka propelling herself from the back of a pew to the top of the organ was worthy of a Discovery Channel documentary. How could such a massive body move so swiftly and deftly? How had this genteel woman managed such a rippling display of physical prowess? The answer, of course, was in the triceps, those great extensor muscles that ran along the backs of her arms: a happy legacy of Milorad Pavlic's military service. The tits might be new, but the musculature that complemented them and added to Zinka's exotic allure was part of the original equipment. For her, such a feat was all in a day's work. For Dean, the inmate she had observed from behind as he made some nefarious deal, it was nothing short of a miracle. Quicker than you can say "in the name of Jesus" he was at her side—or actually at her thighs, as she was rather high up by now—to offer his respects.

"Maybe women should be in the chapel after all, if they can do tricks like that," he said, startling Zinka.

"Now, don't try and butter me up. After you were so nasty." Zinka was surprised by how calm and assured Dean appeared, especially as she had probably caught him doing something illegal. "And lower your voice. We're praying here." Actually, it was Zinka who needed to lower her voice. But the service was already unraveling—coarse whispers, muffled chortles, and the occasional *hola* were audible below—and there was little danger a conversation in the balcony would draw any attention.

"So is that what you're doing, really?" Dean queried leeringly. "Praying, are you?" He rubbed against her thigh and then instinctively pulled away, realizing that if he were ever to get between Zinka's quadriceps, he might never make it out alive. *What was it,* he thought, *about this woman?*

"Don't try anything or I'll write you up," Zinka warned. She was proud she had learned the drill so quickly. From the look on Dean's face, he had already abandoned any inappropriate notions. *Sad, really,* she thought, as she noticed he was quite a looker: large, deep-set green eyes framed by a shaggy mane of glossy hair and a slightly aquiline nose with flaring nostrils. And a body that would fetch millions (of lira, that is) at the meat market on the Piazza Repubblica. Not that she was interested in such things these days. She had her Camille and her reputation. But you can't blame a girl for looking, can you?

Father Brocard gave his homily and, sad to say, it wasn't likely to inspire. Something about love and forgiveness. Well-prepared—probably too well-prepared: It just never took flight. He rarely looked up from his notes and never moved away from the ambo, to which he clung as if for dear life. No one was listening.

The attention of the congregation was riveted to someone else entirely. A hulking Hispanic man of uncommon dignity sat midway up the aisle on the left-hand side—that side of the chapel reserved for the large statue of Our Lady of Guadalupe. The man turned around and quietly addressed a few rows of inmates. He was artfully blocked from Brocard's line of vision by a phalanx of Puertorriqueños, whose obvious purpose was to shield his activities. The respect the inmates should have accorded poor Brocard—the priest, after all—they openly gave this rebel prophet. Zinka could only wonder why.

"That's Willie Acevedo," Dean said, following her gaze. "They call him Bear."

"Not without reason," Zinka heard herself say. She, too, had forgotten Brocard. "And, what, if you don't mind my asking, are they doing down there?"

Dean only smiled. This was his world, and Zinka had to play by his rules. "If you look, really use your eyes, you can figure it out."

Zinka looked hard. In the mass of brown shirts and bobbing heads she noticed that several of the burlier inmates had their arms around the shoulders of the more willowy types. *Nothing too untoward about that,* she thought. Then she noticed that three of these couples appeared to respond to questions Bear asked them. A deep, almost palpable, quasi-religious stillness surrounded the little group. Then, in unison, the three slender men leaned over to rest their heads on the shoulders of the larger men who embraced them. Other men shook hands with the three couples and patted their backs.

"It can't be what I think is it!" Zinka exclaimed. Seeing Dean smile, she added, "Brocard would die."

"Father hasn't the slightest clue what's happening," Dean said. "This is *ñeta* turf. They marry whom they want. They deal what they want. The priest has nothing to say about it."

Zinka decided it was best to let him think the gang was invincible. Poor boy, he had not yet encountered the force of her justice. Or Brocard's surprising cunning.

"But why would macho Hispanics allow, even encourage such things?" Zinka wondered aloud.

Eager to prove how jail-wise he was, Dean appeared willing to tell Zinka anything she asked—to a point, that is. "If any gang member is gay, they have to say so when they join. Then, so they don't play around, especially with Kings or other gang members, they have to get married. They are chosen to be the women of officers." Lest Zinka misunderstand him, he added, "gang officers, that is. They have their own hierarchy."

Zinka was intrigued. "And, if I may ask, is this until death do us part?"

"Good God, no!" It never ceased to amaze Dean how dense people on the street could be. "Just until their stip is up or they max out. It's for convenience, you might say."

So the *ñetas* composed the organization she was looking for. And Willie Acevedo, the Bear, was their leader. Or perhaps it was Dean, who seemed aloof from it all yet very much in control. Could the answer possibly be that simple? Or was this just one more box in a matryushka doll from hell. Every box contained another, and another, and yet another. *Ad infinitum*.

Twenty-One

"BETWEEN US, PRIEST OR NOT, HE'S A MAN." The way she spat out the last word made her sentiments quite clear. "What's more," Tamara Boggs confided to the sister she knew Zinka Pavlic to be, "we both know more than we need to about men, don't we?"

This was not the time for Zinka to tell her new friend how intimately acquainted with the opposite sex she had been. Nor did she have any desire to derail their conversation by confiding to the warden that, even though she far preferred the subtle body of a woman, she was not averse to the occasional bugger. No, it was clear that to get to the truth, a little obfuscation was in order.

"He is a dear, really," Zinka replied, nodding in agreement, "but so very gullible." Ever aware of how people perceived her, and ever prepared to exploit their amazement to her advantage, Zinka unfastened the top buttons of her blouse and leaned over the warden's desk so that her breasts swayed pendulously in front of Tamara Bogg's face. "It feels so good to let these puppies breathe occasionally."

Taken aback by this extraordinary familiarity, the warden could only mouth: "Oh, yes. It must indeed feel good."

To Tamara, who hadn't been this excited since the locker room after undergrad games at Bryn Mawr, Dr. Zinka was all that an ideal woman should be: foreign, intelligent, forward, and stacked, in equal measure. To Zinka, who was fond of chunky dark-complexioned women with attitude, the good warden wasn't half bad either.

"From what I have observed," Zinka continued, "the inmates—how do they put it?—play him out. No doubt you have observed this yourself, clever woman that you are."

Not one to let a compliment go unrecognized, Tamara nodded in agreement, which was Zinka's sign to go in for the kill. "I need one little thing from you in order to see whether these inmates are abusing their privileges. Only then can I know if my program is doing any good, or if they are playing me out as well." Tamara's look said, *Anything you want.* "Telephone records. I want to find out if anyone is using the chaplain's unsecured phone after hours." She read compliance in the warden's eyes. Submission, really.

How could he have been so naive? Perhaps it was just because he was Brocard, the little priest who bumbled his way through life, occasionally, miraculously, getting something right. This was the way everyone, with the sole exception of himself, perceived him. *It might be time,* he thought as he tried to make his way through compline with breviary in hand, *to admit what others have long known.*

It was Zinka, as usual, who precipitated this crisis. She did have a way of bringing everything to a head, a trick of which a passive-aggressive like Father Brocard was constitutionally incapable. When she confronted him the day before about having no control over the inmates, he had to concede that, yes, he was not a disciplinarian and, yes, perhaps they were taking advantage of him somewhat.

"Big time," Zinka had thrown back at him. "They are playing you out, pumpkin."

Brocard was so charmed by being called pumpkin—no one had ever addressed him so affectionately before—that he did not fully understand the gravity of her news.

"If an inmate is making contact with some Mafioso capo, it can only be through an unsecured telephone line. And no one behind bars has access to one of those except you, my precious little *Dummkopf*. There are none at officers' stations or in the social workers' offices. Every telephone but yours goes through the switchboard."

Zinka carefully explained that a tracer had to be installed on his line. To solve the mystery, they needed to know who called whom when. There had to be a record—a list of calls that had been made from the phone.

Though Brocard had spoken highly of Dr. Pavlic to the warden, telling her how this European expert could reshape and energize a rather moribund education program, he was initially doubtful Zinka would be able to get anywhere with her. After all, Tamara Boggs was one of the least cooperative of creatures: a shrew and a misanthrope both. Or so he thought. It did little for his self-esteem when Zinka, flush with success, triumphantly waved the call list in front of him upon her return from her visit with the warden. What charms did she have that he, in his humble goodness, so sorely lacked?

This thought was particularly perplexing as the sound of Zinka's snoring rumbled through throughout the rectory. He saw her now: flat on her back, mouth wide open, nostrils flared, that massive chest expanding and contracting as she tore her way through a rapid succession of dreams. With Zinka, it was one conquest after another.

Aside from her snoring—her least ladylike feature—Brocard had to admit Zinka was a charmer and that without her he would probably get nowhere. He liked to think that his even-tempered way complemented hers and made them a true team. He knew also that, despite her bravado, Zinka was concerned for the truth before any personal acclaim. Anyone who had spent so much psychological and physical energy on getting to the truth of her gender—something so many souls so carelessly take for granted—could be trusted with an investigation like the one they currently pursued. In the house of mirrors called Brotherly Love Pen, someone had to distinguish right from wrong and to make decisions accordingly. He knew that Zinka had touched the truth herself, could vouch for its existence.

Were Zinka the only person to call him naive that day, he might have been able to ignore the charge. But he was twice assaulted with the harsh truth. An E-mail from his testy old friend Avertanus was waiting for Brocard when he returned to his home computer. At first he hoped the missive would provide the diversion he needed to get his mind off the increasingly distressing confusion at Brotherly Love. They had gone through so much together, Brocard and Avertanus. Even their attachment to their absurd religious names united them. Years of study in Rome preceded half a lifetime devoted to the incessant and rather comforting daily routine of monastic life. Even in his retirement in his native Holland, Avertanus kept up with the affairs of the world, including the life of his erstwhile American student. That Brocard cared for and respected Avertanus made his mentor's E-mail even more distressing than it might have been had it come from anyone else.

My Dear Brocard,

This has been a winter of rain. The cemetery beneath my window has turned into a marsh, and I think that any day now, long-departed monks like our old friend Pius might just float to the surface. I honestly don't recall ever seeing so much water, except in those last fateful hours of San Redempto. I often wonder if you lament our lost monastery as much as I do. Especially when I hear about how involved you are in your new criminal environment. You write about it almost as if it were glamorous. I must tell you all of this frightens me, my old friend. Your newfound enthusiasm for such an evil place makes me tremble and causes me to wonder whether you, too, might be drowning.

Let us take these characters you describe one by one, as in a seminar, and see how in your eternal naiveté you might misread them:

Starting with Dean the Nose, I notice how concerned you are that he might be a mastermind of vice. Honestly, my dear friend, does anyone who crouches on all fours to sniff under doors deserve such credit? This misguided lad seems to me so obsessive a personality that he could only follow. Watch him carefully, I say. Observe whom he obsesses over, and you will come near your quarry. End your search with him and you will undoubtedly miss the prize that might well be already in your sight.

Could his obsessive personality point to the delusional Jesucito? The possibility has crossed my mind as I watch the rain fall in sheets against my windowpane and flood the gutter beneath the sill. I did tell you they moved me to the garret, which I infinitely prefer, as it distances me from the infirm old biddies on the second floor. So Jesucito, to get back to him, might well hold the key. His delusion might as easily be used by someone clever; just as sadly, it might lead those weak in mind and faith to follow him as a prophet. See who advances his cause. Keep your eyes open and believe no one. Just look, my old friend. I believe this must be the same person Dean follows as well.

Your clerk Andy is a curious one. I must confess I have not figured him out as you have given him no face. For that matter no flesh and bones. He is at best a chimera, perhaps benign. But why, I ask myself repeatedly, will he not go to Mass? Why does a chapel clerk distance himself from the main activity of the chapel, indeed of all Catholics, since this is what you said he is? I wonder why you have not inquired into this. My thoughts keep going to the devil. (You have to humor me in this my friend. You know how palpable the evil one is for me.) Could he be at work in your clerk? Is it possible that Andy's indifference to both the good and bad, and his marked aversion to Catholic ritual, are signs that the devil has taken possession of his soul?

There is a distinct possibility that none of these characters is anything more than a pawn in a far larger conspiracy. Given your suspicions about the connection between activities at Brotherly Love Pen and the missing Caravaggio nativity, this seems a reasonable conjecture. In any event, these three are, to use detective parlance, your prime suspects. However, it would be a grave mistake to end your investigation with them. Continue to look at the officers and be particularly attentive to that Hispanic gang you mentioned. Above all, be alert and do not allow yourself to be deceived. In that pestilent place where you minister there is a force at work that might well destroy all goodness. Even yours. Do keep me abreast of your investigation and please, do take care of yourself.

—Your Brother in Christ, Avertanus

As Brocard's eyes grew heavy, he welcomed the rest that would come with sleep. Sooner than he could ever have imagined, the time would come when he would have to keep his eyes wide open as he walked headlong into the belly of the beast.

Twenty-Two

MIDWAY ON HIS JOURNEY THROUGH LIFE, Father Brocard found himself lost and afraid. Not hopelessly lost, as it turned out. Unaccustomed to driving in the dark, he had taken a wrong turn in the woods surrounding the prison complex and ended up approaching it from an unfamiliar side. Nor was he completely seized with fear. A mild trembling, a muted apprehension shook him when he saw for the first time the rows of razor wire and the armed guard towers surrounding the Big Yard. His normal approach to Brotherly Love took him up the main drive into a spacious parking lot, then through a well-manicured garden and into the rather inviting lobby. His wrong turn brought him to the peripheral road and gave him a more accurate view of where he was: a place of punishment and sin where forgiveness was as rare as retribution was common.

An unsettling and not entirely unexpected silence hung over

Brotherly Love—considering it was nearly midnight. By that hour, inmates were to be locked down for the night. (As should have been a morning person like Brocard.) A novice master who waxed poetic about such things had taught him the night was the devil's preferred time. Then chaos, not order, reigned; shadows distorted the beauty of creation and evil found nurture in the dark.

Unannounced and unaccompanied, Brocard planned to wander the facility to discover what he might be missing in the glare of day. Even though he had no idea what to expect and had told himself that nothing would surprise him, he was taken aback by the scene that greeted him in the lobby. Sergeant Kraus, at her most officious, ran about shouting orders to the third shift building-service inmate crew.

"Get more buckets out of the J.C. closet! Hurry!" she bellowed. Water surged from one of the air vents on the wall and a virtual river deepened around the main gate. "Don't just stand there looking. Mop it up! *Dummkopf!* Empty out that bucket there! Move it!"

Brocard had never seen anyone's eyes blaze as brightly, nor any skin turn as gray with anxiety, as Sergeant Kraus's did that night. She had taken on the part of Charon: through her and her alone might one win safe passage through the gates of Brotherly Love Pen.

"It's late, Father," she said, wild-eyed. "The whole place is falling apart. Better for you to go home."

Her tone was agitated but firm, even motherly, in a storm trooper kind of way. However, Brocard was on a mission, and he would not be deterred by a little water.

"I'm sorry to bother you at this late hour, Sergeant," (Why did he always find himself apologizing for everything?). "But there are some inmates I have to check in on."

"At this hour? Jesus, Father, give the boys a rest." Then, seeing he was not going to budge and realizing he had every right to be there, as irregular as the hour might be, she waved him through the metal detector and stepped to his side.

"Now, take my arm," she commanded. "I've got my boots on and you have those flimsy loafers. If any one is going to fall flat on their ass we both know who it will be. I don't want broken bones on my beat."

As they made their way slowly through the pooling water, he heard screams, possibly howls, somewhere in the distance. "The assholes are going crazy tonight," she remarked flatly. Then, as if more explanation were needed, she told him the main boiler was out and that an auxiliary boiler was working overtime. In consequence, parts of the prison were arctic while others were unbearably hot. "They're acting up," she concluded. "Just pretending they are suffering or something. Probably just want to get a lawsuit out of this mess. I know these scumbags, Father."

After they made it through the two gates that separated the lobby from the entrance hallway, Kraus suggested he avoid the outer houses. He should try to make his rounds, if he still wanted to, upstairs in the dormitory area where the weather was tropical and the inmates were probably less anxious. Brocard knew that if he expected to see what was truly happening he would have to forge on, deeper into the complex. But, with the ever-solicitous Kraus watching, he decided it was best to take her advice and head for the dorms.

Brotherly Love was a sprawling complex: It looked not unlike a giant squid from the air. Center Control was a glassed-in domed area from which the tentacles radiated. At the end of the first of these arms was the dormitory: an enormous, featureless chamber with all the charm, well, of a prison.

It surprised Brocard how little stir his visit caused. To him there was something extraordinary about an impromptu appearance. People hardly noticed him. To be sure, officers nodded hello before returning to their monitors and occasionally inmates looked up from the flick books barely concealed under their covers. But that was it. He realized no one feared him. In the eyes of all, his presence was truly insignificant.

The heat in the dormitory was unbearable. Hell itself could not compete. The brutal temperature was taking its toll on many of the inmates, some of whom screamed madly at the guards to turn down the fucking heat. (Brocard also noticed that his presence did nothing to soften the expletives.) He wondered whether they were laying it on deliberately to insult him. The Caribbeans, accustomed to the swelter, were in their element. They bared their pumped-up chests, tied back their hair, and displayed their tattoos as if they were selling themselves on Condato Beach. This was their house and their time. The oppressive heat did nothing more than make them glisten.

A group of nearly 20 inmates gathered in the far corner. When he got nearer to them, he noticed they were in the thrall of Bear. He spoke to them with a quiet, charismatic voice of authority. Calling upon his Italian, Brocard had no real difficulty understanding Bear's words. Beyond his comprehension was how the authorities could remain oblivious to the group's seditious activities.

Ustedes se encargan del pedido de quinientos paquetes que llegan hoy por la puerta. Y del alcohol mañana-doscientas botellas de ron y otras doscientas de whisky.

Brocard was stunned: 500 crates of cigarettes being delivered that night, and several hundred bottles of alcohol tomorrow. No mention of drugs at that point, but Brocard had little doubt these too were part of their empire. The scale of their operation and its brazenness astounded him. It was clear that Bear and his *ñetas* knew Brocard overheard their plans. It was also clear they felt in no way threatened by him. In fact, Bear continued to tell his posse where everything was to be stored and how they were to distribute the contraband.

Finally, the business over, Bear condescendingly signaled for Father Brocard to come forward. He shook Brocard's hand and presented him as a prize to his officers. When Brocard turned and looked at them, faces he had seen often at Mass, some of whose names he even knew, they were almost unrecognizable to him. In the heat of that night and in the fervor of that moment, he could only see gluttons: the spenders and the hoarders who peopled the first circle of hell. They slaked their desires by amassing more, no matter the consequences and no matter the human cost. Their lives were reduced to nothing more than stuff; all other values were forgotten. And yet, as Bear placed one of his massive paws on his shoulder, Brocard understood they looked on him as one of their own. This, above everything else he had seen and heard, disturbed him most.

"Father Brocard," Bear said, switching into English out of respect for the priest, "we know we can trust you because you are a man of God. We are people of God. We are the ones who execute God's justice here in this place and all places like it."

"It is good to hear you say you are people of God but…" Brocard caught himself. Was this really the time to confront this matter? Could he say or do anything to change the way things were? All that stood between him and a couple of hundred inmates, many of whom presumably listened to the Borinqueño towering at his side, was one semicomatose officer watching infomercials in a cage 50 yards away. No, now was not the time to wage war with evil. Rather, his task was to observe the enemy so that he might deal with him more adroitly in the future.

"Well, men," Brocard said, giving a little wave and extricating himself from the Bear's grasp, "I will no doubt see you all at Mass this weekend. And always remember, if there is anything you want to talk about, my door is always open." Feeling remarkably weak, as much from the rising heat as from the meeting he had inadvertently stumbled into, Brocard made his way out toward the guard post. He had wanted to say a few words to the officer on duty, really just to register shock about what was happening right before his eyes. But the droning of the television had worked its magic, and the guard was contentedly twitching his way through some dream which, in God's compassionate wisdom, allowed him to escape the tedium and danger his job entailed.

The smell of chili and a cooling temperature drew Brocard to Center Control. Stomachs might be rumbling and boilers might be going wacko everywhere else, but the third-shift lieutenant was not to suffer. And, interestingly, the inmate who was tending to his needs, running to and from kitchen, was no other than Dean.

"You certainly do get around, Mr. Dean," Brocard remarked icily.

"Anywhere I want," Dean answered defiantly. "You can't even keep me out of your blessed little chapel now, can you? It's in the code, you know. I have my rights."

"And privileges, it seems." Brocard watched Dean tuck into a large container of chili—his reward for supplying the lieutenant and his officers with food. It wasn't easy getting the kitchen help to muster something special at one in the morning. But Dean had a juice card, as they say in jail: his way of getting whatever he wanted.

Just then, Brocard heard keys rattling behind him. He so wished people in Brotherly Love would wear leather soles. His nerves were fragile, and this sneaking around had to stop.

"I just double-checked the chapel area," Officer Thomas said to the startled priest. "All secured, you will be happy to know."

Officer Thomas was on movement control. More significantly, this meant Thomas had keys to Brocard's office throughout the night. When and how had this come about? He tried to maintain his composure, but it was clear that Officer Thomas's appearance had rattled him.

"You surprised me, Officer." Brocard tried unsuccessfully to be composed. "I never realized you were on this post. Guess I always associated you with Ad Seg."

"Overtime," Thomas said flatly. "Need the money for a mission down in the islands. God's work."

There they go, dragging poor God into things again. Brocard knew, as did everyone else, that Thomas was swimming in gambling debts. The ruse of religion might work with a few inmates, but not for him. Still, this night was for seeing, not acting.

Obvious even to Brocard was the unholy alliance between Dean and Officer Thomas. It was not just that both of them hid behind an exceedingly narrow and judgmental biblical faith. More importantly, they had a common purpose. From the looks they exchanged, it was clear they were coconspirators in a scheme far more dangerous than small-minded interpretation of Scripture.

Realizing he would get nowhere with either of them and wanting to move on, Brocard ventured into another tentacle of the prison, toward the sally port, the area where deliveries arrived and garbage departed. On his way, he passed an old black officer, stooped with years and gray with worry, whom he had seen around often but never before spoken with.

"Excuse me, Father," the officer said. Brocard paused and gave him his attention. "I don't want to get you upset or anything, but watch out, will you, Father? You're a good man, I can tell. We don't get too many of them in here, so they sort of stand out, if you know what I mean. It's just that that office of yours is wide open at night. They can do whatever they want, if you get my gist. You can get yourself in a heap of trouble and that wouldn't be right."

Before Brocard could say a word, the officer was gone. Even the snakes, he thought, wanted to protect him from evil. Whoever this man was, Brocard was thankful for him. Of course, his office was wide open. There was nothing to prevent wrongdoers from using his computer and unprotected telephone after hours. In fact, with Dean wandering freely, and Officer Thomas in charge of the keys, he would be an idiot to think otherwise. He could only wonder what chaos these demons had unleashed and how widespread it had become.

Brocard was almost relieved to encounter Andy and Cavallo at the sally port. Because Andy had made no secret about it, Brocard knew that his clerk volunteered as a runner for the officers at night. It seemed like a perfect match for an insomniac. And it took no brains to figure out that on this of all nights, with the heating system going crazy, Cavallo would be in great demand. What did surprise Brocard was how attached Cavallo seemed to be to Andy: like a puppy to its mother or, to use Zinka's more earthy phrase, like a bootlicking slave to his master. The relationship took him aback. But by now this new revelation couldn't faze him much.

"Late night, huh, Father?" As usual, Andy was unflappable. In the middle of a major drug deal, he would have been as dispassionate and courteous as ever.

"Just making the rounds," Brocard replied. "Thought I would see how you all were weathering the climate changes." As he was saying this, Brocard noticed that Cavallo was upset by his presence. Brocard felt he had interrupted the inmate in the midst of saying or doing something important.

"So, what are you two up to anyway?" he queried. Small talk was not Brocard's strong suit. More often than not, conversations simply ground to a halt when he tried his hand at easy banter. Still, being trained in big city ways, Andy could easily deflect silliness with silliness.

"We're just taking in the smells of the sally port," he said gamely. "You know, something to do on a winter's night when the boilers are exploding all around." After making his little speech, Andy told Cavallo, with a smirk and a subtle move of his head— could it be lovers' speech?—that it was time for him to get back to work.

"Yeah," Cavallo muttered. "They're having some heating problems over in the hospital area. So they want me to look at it, I guess." Then, taking another cue from Andy, Cavallo suggested to Brocard that perhaps the priest ought to come to the hospital with him. There was someone there whom he might want to see.

It was not necessary to say goodbye to Andy. Prisons didn't work that way. In fact, most social courtesies were best left at the gate. Hellos and goodbyes made little sense in a place where time stretched out amorphously and resisted the usual means of marking its passage.

The temperature dropped precipitously as Brocard followed Cavallo, his plumbing tools in tow, down the tentacle that led to the hospital. By the time they arrived, frost had begun to form on the bulletproof glass surrounding the officer's station. And Nurse Francine, plump and unusually jovial for such a place and time, revealed only her sparkling eyes. The rest of her was swaddled in arctic gear.

"Well, isn't this a fine fare-thee-well?" she chortled. "Is that the expression I want? Well, anyway, my patients are slipping into deep-freeze. I do hope you have come to pray for the boiler's rapid recovery, Father. Otherwise, no telling what we are going to do now, is there?"

"You could let me work on it," Cavallo said softly but firmly. "I am the plumber, after all." Brocard had never seen Cavallo speak up for himself. Forthrightness rather agreed with him.

Nothing like a little righteous indignation to bring out the best in a man—even an oversexed felon.

Never one to register put-downs or to dwell on the negative, Francine told Brocard how delighted she was that he had stopped by. Third shift, which she had drawn more times than she could remember, tended to get very dull. And there was an inmate who had been rushed to the hospital who needed the counsel of a chaplain. He was a religious type—a bit fanatical, in fact. From what she could tell, he had ingested some razor blades, thinking that was a good way to cut out the devil who lived within. Understandably he had passed out. But he was coming to and it was probably a good time for Brocard to pay him a visit. Checking the chart, Francine read out a series of Latin names, then added, "but everyone seems to refer to him as 'Jesucito.'"

How could Father Brocard tell anyone, especially the ebullient Francine, that there were limits to his compassion? Especially at, by now, two in the morning? Brocard did not relish the prospect of consoling an inmate who viewed him as the anti-Christ. Nevertheless, as she drifted off into the bitter night, he assured Francine that he would look in on Jesucito. What more could he do? He had heard that Jesucito had embarked on a 40-day fast and had decided to wage total war on the "fiend." Now 20 pounds lighter, balls crushed, and intestines lacerated, he had become the poster boy for ill-begotten born-again homegrown fundamentalism. Short of drugs—and lots of them—there was little more Brocard thought he could do to help the poor boy. So, when he poked his nose in to check on the inmate, Brocard was quite relieved to see that Jesucito was still fast asleep. He had done his job, kept his promise to Francine. It was time to move on. There were surely other things to discover.

Once again, as he had done during Brocard's nocturnal visit, Cavallo assumed the role of Virgil. With barely a word uttered between them, Brocard followed Cavallo to an open grating in the hospital floor and down a ladder to a subterranean passage.

"Most people," Cavallo said slowly, "they live here, they work here, and they never know this place exists." He was clearly pleased to reveal a whole new world to the priest. Brocard, whose eyes were getting rather tired of revelations, would have been quite content to live in ignorance. As interesting as it might be to plumbers, the fundament of Brotherly Love was a dark, cold, and forbidding place.

For Cavallo, on the other hand, this was a virtual garden of delights. How many times had he gotten blown in these corridors? How many asses had he satisfied? No, for Cavallo, there was nothing threatening about these dank passages. For him, they meant freedom and happiness.

They made their way to the boiler, where they met up with a maintenance crew feverishly at work. By now it was clear that Brocard had taken a wrong turn. A middle-aged priest had no business being underground at a prison in the wee hours of the morning.

Cavallo led him to another ladder, then through an open grating that emptied into the Big Yard. The beauty of the stars, like the vision that had greeted Dante at the end of his harrowing journey, refreshed Brocard's soul more fully than any other nighttime sky he had ever beheld. A chill passed through him as he considered how far he had traveled into the bowels of the Inferno. And while part of him was amused by his overly dramatic perspective on a lackluster gang of small-time cons in a forgotten jail, another more reasonable part of him was pleased he had finally opened his eyes to reality.

Twenty-Three

"ART ALONE—LISTEN CAREFULLY TO WHAT I AM SAYING—art alone matters, my silly little cleric. Everything else, and I mean everything, is merely a distraction." Zinka was becoming untethered, and it was not for Brocard to pull her in. Anyway, in his own rather masochistic way, he rather liked to see her flying about and ranting, even at him. There was something both invigorating and comforting about it: almost maternal, in a Medean sort of way. "Yes, I have no doubt you have seen closets full of cigarettes and hooch." (She played with and truly loved the elongated vowels— what Serb wouldn't, after all? — in that silly American word). "No doubt there are warehouses full of condoms, too, judging from the way these boys hump. And from the lustful way I've seen them all looking at me…" Here she digressed, as was often the case, to wonder what it was about her that made men go crazy. Brocard nearly remarked that it was a combination of an inflated ego and an equally inflated bosom. But seasoned cleric that he was, he wisely held his tongue.

"The *Palermo Caravaggio*," Zinka began when she got back on track, "is all that should matter to us. Once we locate that, all these other pieces will fall in place. And if we fail to find it—I'm saying this to make my point, for I don't believe for a second we will not succeed—then who gives a hoot?" (Ah, those vowels again!) "A hoot, I say."

Then, turning to Brocard, she expelled him from his office. "Now be a nice little priest and leave me alone for a tad. Go out and save some souls or something. Just leave Zinka alone with this computer of yours. If I can believe my newfound woman's intuition, it has secrets to tell."

Brocard was reluctant to leave. His downcast eyes and hunched shoulders told her, *It's my office, after all.*

"All right, then," she said, relenting. "If you insist on staying, stand out in the hallway and keep watch. Even though it is time for count and those inquisitive little inmates are supposed to be in their cells, there's no telling who might manage to con their way out of count and into our affairs." Brocard was impressed by Zinka's study of prison-speak. She was like a sponge, soaking up everything and everyone in sight. "Now, to work!"

Somehow Brocard had imagined Zinka would start by pulling a chair up to the monitor and turning on the switch. But, as he should have guessed, the conventional was never her style. No, Zinka flopped belly-down on the floor like a marine about to push a quick 50 and then, hitching up her skirt as she wedged herself under Brocard's desk, she began to inspect the back of the CPU.

"Hello! What do we have here?" she exclaimed.

"Zinka, please," Brocard said with pique. "Not that Sherlock Holmes thing again. I am not your Watson."

"You are no fun, no fun at all," Zinka replied teasingly. Then, after a long pause interspersed with a couple of judicious grunts, she decided to can the suspense and tell him what she had found. "I had thought you said there was no modem in this computer."

"There is none. It was taken out when the computer was brought to my office."

"Well," Zinka replied, "someone has stuck it back in, my dear little innocent. They do things like that in jail, I believe. Lie and deceive. They're even good at it, from all I hear." Having found the port, she had only to pry Andy's desk open and rummage around for the briefest period of time before she located the telephone jack. In one deft movement she turned on the computer, hooked up the jack, and began searching for the Internet connection. Nothing as crass as an icon, but really easy enough to find in a quick search of the hard drive.

She's good, Brocard thought to himself. *And I truly was naive. Probably still am.*

Sure enough, the server number was the very one that had been accessed after hours on Brocard's telephone—God bless the horny warden. And as for the main addressee, it was none other than CAPO123, from the cryptic note Brocard had found in the choir loft. Everything pointed to one man and one place: Don Pepe in Vico Equense.

By now Zinka had broken out into a full sweat—no dainty glow for her. Rivulets dripped off her face and chest and poured into her cleavage.

Everything was clear now. Andy's time in the office was too limited for him to have done anything as foolhardy as this. But Dean had access to the office and was as stupid as he was bold. Zinka and Brocard had connected the dots. Now, ever so cautiously, they had to go in for the kill.

Twenty-Four

WHITE BOYS DON'T SING SPIRITUALS. Especially Eurocentric middle-aged white boys. Even though Brocard instinctively knew this, he could not get the old slave-song out of his mind, no matter how hard he tried. Interestingly, he had first heard it in Rome. Kathleen Battle, ever the rebel, had performed one as an encore at the end of her all-Mozart recital at Santa Cecilia. Even now, it was hard for him to convey the illicit shock he had experienced in that moment. "Precious Lord, Take My Hand" was one of those turgid Baptist lines that swelled in sound and meaning, only to deflate into the hopelessness of the present. He might have forgotten her performance and the song, if Cuchifrito had not selected it as his anthem. Feeling particularly oppressed by a homophobic guard, he hummed it under his breath incessantly. And when the occasion arose, he sang it plaintively in full voice, as he had that morning when he was helping the porters strip and wax the chapel floors. Now, with everyone gone for count, Brocard found himself alone and unable to shake the song's reverberations.

His problem was not that he wanted to rid himself of the melody, as if it were simply an intrusive jingle. Rather, he was habitually unable to remember any lyrics past the first line. Not the case with *"Salve Regina"* or *"Alma Redemtoris Mater,"* of course. What monk worth his salt could forget even a syllable of those? No, the words to secular songs and vernacular hymns simply failed to lodge in any retrievable brain cells. And this drove him crazy.

So down he went into the chapel—cautiously, as the floor was freshly waxed—in search of one of the Baptist hymnals. Fortunately, he remembered the second line—"I am tired, I am weak, I am worn"—which summed up rather well the state that his experiences these last few days had put him in. The eye-opening midnight wander and then Zinka's embarrassing discovery had brought him to a point where he didn't know what to think or whom, if anyone, to trust. He recalled Avertanus's list of possible culprits and struggled hard to shake his old friend's rather occult suspicions. Determined to be realistic and observant, he believed everything pointed as clearly as any cliché to the Nose, to Dean, and no one else.

It was this conviction more than anything else that set him up for his next shock. After rummaging fruitlessly through the vestment closet and sacristy, he remembered that some of the old Baptist hymnals had been thrown into the immersion tub (or as he too had begun to refer to it, the Jacuzzi) after the Pentecostal volunteers' last dousing. A snippet of lyrics dashed through his mind, something like "hear my cry, hear my call"— and then the word "fall" prophetically came back to him as he made his way over to the large wooden box along the back wall of the chapel.

The first sign that something was amiss: someone had moved the pots of poinsettia from Christmases past that normally sat on the wooden lid. Brocard's hope that Beto the porter had finally jettisoned the grim foliage was quickly dashed when he caught sight of the pots neatly lined up by the stair to the choir loft. Perhaps Cuchifrito had looked for the hymnals there as well. Someone, it seems, had wanted to get them.

Fearing nothing—years in Rome do have a way of inuring one to danger— he threw the lid open and peered inside. The sight of a corpse plunged him into shock. He suddenly remembered the words he had been looking for: "Hold my hand, lest I fall." He quietly said them as a prayer.

Dead bodies were not new to Father Brocard, of course. But, as he peered into the appropriately coffin-shaped box, he could not help being impressed by the sadistic care with which this one had been trussed: feet and arms tied back like a turkey, shirt opened to the navel to expose the white meat, and a plastic bag meticulously tied over the head to ensure that suffocation would be complete and swift. Even in the dim light he recognized Dean. And, as he stared down at the corpse, Brocard's new problem became blazingly clear. Internal affairs would be called in, an investigation would place the chapel under surveillance, and— worst of all—his work with Zinka was back to square one.

He did manage to locate the hymnals. Taking one out and closing the lid, he found the words he was looking for and filled the chapel with his song: "At the river I stand. Guide my feet, hold my hand. Take my hand, Precious Lord. Lead me home."

Twenty-Five

THEY HAD TO WALK; OTHERWISE, HOW COULD THEY THINK? For once, they both knew exactly how peripatetic Greek philosophers must have felt. As Zinka so aptly put it, "Let's move it. The blood is pooling in my ass!" So they flung open the doors to the rectory, where they had been catatonically musing on their fate, and ventured out into the final onslaught of winter's fury. Their agora was no colonnaded marble pile but rather severe and lushly planted Bryn Mawr College. The curious scholars who clustered around them as they strolled were, to a person, young and bright-eyed women. The composition of this audience would have surely unsettled Aristotle, but it delighted Zinka and Brocard to no end. They weren't the only ones amused.

What a strikingly absurd couple they made. Zinka, larger in life than in the telling, was draped in the pelts of some endangered species, her massive body balanced precariously on stilettos that on the wrong feet could kill. Brocard's head was covered with a beret so battered and misshapen that it just had to have a story, which it did. His body was concealed by a monastic cape so full that it billowed, as if at full sail, as they walked along. He was as compact as she was large, as pensive as she was effusive. Yet they were joined in their deep concern for what had happened and what they had to do next. This obsession set them apart from the callow undergraduates, who were busy perfecting their poses of studied indifference.

"It was all so clear when Dean was the prime suspect," Brocard lamented.

"It was too easy," Zinka mused. "As is presuming it's Andy alone. There has to be more to it." For Zinka, there was something exhilarating about thinking out loud. She even read under her breath when she researched—a practice that infuriated the more introverted bookworms who usually haunted her favorite libraries.

"Our mistake has been not pulling back the lens, like one of those long shots your beloved Hitchcock used to take." Here she stopped to outstretch her arms and expose her ample cleavage, so as to take in the whole world and quite a few of the sisters nearby. "Pull back, I say. Pull back. We have focused on a mere detail and missed the picture."

Being a ruminator and a slow one at that, Brocard was still stuck on the simile. "Do you mean," he said after a considerable pause, "the aerial shots Alfred Hitchcock takes at the beginning and ends of films. First, the whole town, then—"

"Oh, do shut up and listen," Zinka interjected. "I'm on to something here." Smiling broadly at a lone freshman riveted by the sheer drama that was Zinka—admirers must always be dealt with graciously—she secured her fur against the cold, slipped her arm around the bewildered priest's, and led him onward. "Maybe the officers have something to do with this. I know how you hate to question authority, but there it is. Maybe the trouble lies with the officers, or maybe a combination of gang activity and officers, or some other permutation. What is important here, my little pumpkin, is that we have three murders." She felt his body tense. "Don't get spasmodic on me, just listen. Three murders and no immediate suspects—just a clear connection to a Mafia boss and a Caravaggio painting that we both long to get our hands on. Which leads me to one path of action and only one."

"Can we get back to the three murders, please?" Brocard pleaded. "Perhaps there were, but still—"

"Hush, my meticulous melon. Details, remember. Pull the camera back."

"To where? Is it possible for me at least to know that?" *Exasperating woman*, Brocard thought.

"My darling, it is so clear. I need to find the most devious art dealer in Naples and through him reach out to our elusive Mafioso. You, of course, being a homebody by nature, will stay in jail. Years of monastic training have prepared you for that at least."

She was right, of course. Zinka always was. It was time for them to take a different approach to this byzantine affair. He would mind the shop; she would fly off to confront danger.

Suddenly, Zinka drew to a halt—their walk was over. They had arrived at the building that housed the art department and the office of her lecherous old friend, Professor Mitchum. "*In bocca al lupo*," she said to Brocard as she kissed him on both cheeks and sent him on his way. In this game it was sometimes difficult to distinguish the prey from the predator.

Twenty-Six

THE CONTRAST BETWEEN THE TWO OF THEM AT THAT moment could not have been starker. And what they did next dictated their respective paths and determined their subsequent actions. They were, of course, simply playing their parts, living in character. As it turned out, that is what eventually secured their success.

Left alone, Brocard was overwhelmed by the amount of information assaulting him. It was as if he saw everything too clearly. Phalanxes of starlings plunged through the early evening sky as the setting sun caught the yellow buds of new leaves on neatly ordered rows of elms. Young women swirled around him on their way to dining halls, study sessions, or illicit liaisons. Gone were those monkish days when he practiced custody of the eyes. Ever fascinated by life, he missed nothing and he missed everything: little Brocard.

He saw Zinka's abrupt departure as an opportunity to open his eyes to all that was happening at Brotherly Love. With his clearer vision, he hoped new patterns of activity and new potential culprits might surface. If he left now, he would be back at the prison after mess cleared. Inmates would be going out to evening shops; the kitchen cleanup crews would be on. There would be much to observe and to learn. He could not expand his vision globally, as his friend Zinka planned to do, but with the patience of a Pasteur, he could place his evil boys under a microscope to observe their every wiggle and determine their hidden laws. Galvanized by this thought, he secured his cape at the neck and marched through quadrangles, under arches, and over trestles to his car. He now had a plan and he longed to execute it.

For Zinka, the need to open her lens (and not just her legs) to the whole world required laser precision. Each step along her expansive new route required the sure knowledge of where she was going, why, and with whom. No matter how dangerous or sordid her mission (and she truly hoped to encounter plenty of danger and sordidness), she was prepared to risk everything (what art historian wouldn't, after all?) to retrieve a lost Caravaggio nativity. No one who beheld her as she stood imperiously in the doorway of the Graduate Art History Room, waiting for everyone to drop everything and do her bidding, could doubt her stature and determination. All were prepared to do her bidding.

"May I help you?" a student worker inquired.

"What a darling you are." Zinka oozed charm as she lowered her coat over her shoulders and pretended to be interested in her surroundings. "Is Professor Mitchum in?"

"Well, yes, he is, but he is awfully busy." The young researcher turned somewhat colder, as if she had been given instructions to keep all visitors at bay. At this, one of those rare men who manage to elbow his way into Bryn Mawr Graduate School got up from his terminal and came over to help Zinka.

"The professor is trying to meet a deadline for an article," the boy began, "and has told us that he is not to be disturbed under any circumstances." The poor lad's voice cracked as he tried to sound authoritative.

"Just tell him it is Professoressa Zinka Pavlic from Paris and Rome," she replied.

At this a third student came to attention. From the look on their awestruck faces they hadn't the slightest clue who she was, but they were mortified to think that their cluelessness betrayed their ignorance.

Seeing she was getting nowhere, and knowing she had far to go, she pushed past them and headed toward the clearly marked office. "Oh, never mind," she huffed. "Just take my coat—there's a good little boy. And get back to your Panovsky, the lot of you!"

"Mitchum, where are you?" she bellowed. She closed the door firmly behind her, not wanting to upset the students any more than she already had. "You can't hide from me forever."

She heard a bump under the desk and knew she had located the hapless academic.

"If you are going to jerk off at the sheer excitement of seeing me again, do me the courtesy of allowing me to observe the proceedings." Exactly how such an act could be considered a courtesy was clear only to Zinka herself.

Mustering what little dignity he had left, Mitchum slowly crept from under his desk. The long strands of an unruly comb-over popped up in clown-like fashion. A couple of pats from the Professor's moistened hands did little to tame them. And his eyes, whose puffiness had in former days given him a "bedroom" cuteness, were all but hidden by bags and discoloration. He was, quite simply, a wreck of a man: the remains of a life of unbridled debauchery and privilege.

"The last time I saw you," Mitchum said, trying to gain the high ground, "you were lying flat on your back in Malouf's Gallery in Paris with your tits bouncing in the breeze."

As any mention of her breasts filled Zinka with unabashed pride, she took no offense.

"And, as I recall, you were being taken off by the gendarmes for questioning," she replied. She smiled, almost seductively, as she glided to the armchair in front of his desk and eased her way into it. For the life of him, Mitchum could not imagine why this harpy, whom he had once found curiously attractive, had forced her way back into his life. Still, she was on his turf now and, starting to feel somewhat more at ease, he decided to hear her out. Knowing the Professoressa as he did, he suspected she was up to something interesting.

"Let's cut to the chase, Mitchum," she said. "I need a favor, and by my calculations, you owe me a big one."

Before leaving his office she told him not to get up. Under his obsessive gaze, she slowly went over to him, leaned down, pressed her breasts into his face and held him firmly there with both her hands so that all he could see, feel, and smell was Zinka.

Then she picked up and folded the paper with the information he had provided and blew him a kiss. Always mindful of the role she played in men's lives, she lowered her voice and offered one command before turning to leave.

"You can unzip now, Professor. Enjoy yourself."

Twenty-Seven

BROCARD ARRIVED AS AUTO-BODY, UPHOLSTERY, and other evening shops were called for some inmates and as special medications (to keep a lid on things at night) were dispensed to others. His plan was to stay until he discovered some new part of the puzzle, however long that might take. By now he was firmly convinced there were more players and more angles than he had yet considered. As it turned out, this was a nearly fatal miscalculation. His first surprise that evening was finding the main door to the chapel area locked and cordoned off. Bivings, the officer on movement control, was extremely apologetic about having to bar him from his chapel. She was a good Christian, after all—at least that is what she repeatedly told him. He had no desire to doubt her or, quite honestly, even to find out. He just wanted to get into his office to gather some things and then to make his rounds. Though, in truth, he wanted more than that. He needed to know whether his office had been swagged, like the cell of any common criminal. Had Internal Affairs gotten their nose into things? And if so, how far had they gone? Bivings suggested he see the chief, who happened to be working late because of all the goings on. Without orders from above, Bivings "couldn't do nothing," as she averred.

Brocard's answer was to come sooner than he had expected. As it happened, Chief Janochek had the head of internal affairs in his office when Brocard arrived. Inspector Dufoe, an impressive-looking woman with the bearing of a high-priced maîtresse and the credentials to match, paced the room, with a sheaf of papers in hand, obviously trying to make sense of something. And obviously getting nowhere.

"Father Brocard—exactly the person we needed to see." The chief's demeanor in no way matched his words. The whole mess involving the chapel—especially the trussed corpse in the Jacuzzi—had upset an otherwise cushy job. Like most of the administrators hired by Prison World, the chief was a retired state employee who had bailed when his workload increased and his benefits diminished. The private company got him cheap, of course, which was how such an organization justified its very existence. But, as the saying goes, they got what they paid for. In his two years at Brotherly Love Pen, the only significant decision he had made was to replace the trousers in his wardrobe with Sans-a-belt slacks. A rite of passage for seniors—though not the kind of decisive action one usually associated with people entrusted to supervise felons. Sad to say, during Janochek's tenure as chief of Custody at Brotherly Love, the only things that grew substantially were his butt and his stock portfolio. And he had liked that just fine, as he was wont to say. That is, until business at the chapel began to unravel. "Inspector Dufoe here has a few questions about things over there in your religion area, which I would be grateful if you would clear up."

"Father Brocard," the inspector began, "we haven't formally met, but no doubt you know who I am." Did she mean, Brocard wondered, that he had likely heard the rumors about her prior adventures in New Jersey, where she had been found guilty of sexually harassing a male officer? Could she mean, Brocard speculated as he took the seat she offered, the rumors that she planted shanks and gang materials in the cells of inmates whom she wanted to transfer to Prison World's new (and half-empty) maximum-security facility near Pittsburgh?

"Of course I know you, Inspector," seemed the most truthful, and least contentious, response Brocard could make.

"You are probably aware by now, Father Brocard, that we have had to seal off the chapel area for our investigation." Corrupt as she might be, Inspector Dufoe knew her role and played it perfectly. "I have here hard copies of correspondence we took from your computer." The chief imperiously raised a finger to silence Brocard, lest he try to interrupt the inspector. "Were you aware, Father, that the computer you had been given special permission to have in your office was equipped with an illegal modem? Let me remind you: in complete contradiction to the orders that you were given."

"I'm not sure about the contradiction, Inspector," he replied. Seeing she was upset at his response, Brocard tried to clarify. "Now, if you said 'in complete disregard of the orders' or even, perhaps, 'in willful opposition,' then I would understand what you're trying to say." How could he say, pedant that he was, that police-speak drove him crazy? Just say what you have to say. Who on earth used "contradiction" this way anyway?

"Father Brocard," Inspector Dufoe said, lowering her voice and trying to disguise her displeasure, "just how much of the sex chat-room antics were you aware of? Tell me that."

This was a turn that he had not expected. E-mails to Mafiosos and possibly even assassination plots he had fully expected, but not this. Realizing he had to say something, but not wanting to give away the store, he threw the inspector a bone.

"I had just found out about the modem, Inspector, which was part of my reason for coming in tonight. The only reason I had not gone directly to the warden about it is that, frankly, I wanted to be able to tell her something substantive—for example, why it was put in and by whom."

"And which one of these young felons do you have your eye on, Father?" the chief asked coolly. Brocard was somewhat surprised to hear the chief spring back to life. Though not half as surprised as the chief was to hear what Brocard next said.

"Not one of the inmates, Chief. Not alone, anyway. It seems to me it has to be one of the officers, and to narrow it down even more, an officer on the third shift. I know for a fact they have used my office telephone at night."

"And how do you know that, Father?" the inspector interjected. Now it was she who was annoyed.

"Because some mornings it is not in the exact place I left it the night before." Seeing they both doubted him, he added, "I am quite compulsive about certain things. From the breviary on my night table to the arrangement of things on my desk top, everything has an exact place—as Pythagoras would say, a harmony of place—and I know immediately when something has been tampered with."

A wall of silence—the proverbial blue wall—descended. Afterward, all the inspector had to say was that Internal Affairs would take over the entire matter and that, while Brocard would have access to his office and the chapel area, he would notice some changes. More sinister still, there were more changes to come, which he was just going to have to learn how to live with. She regarded the priest with the wry smile of a dominatrix.

At least he had permission to return to his office. Which, as it turned out, was a mixed blessing. Inspector Dufoe and her cohorts were nothing if not thorough. Surveying the disaster, he saw why she had smiled when he remarked how compulsive he was. After her swag of his office, absolutely nothing was where it should have been. Some things, like his computer and answering machine, had been completely removed.

He stood for several minutes at the door trying to assess the damage. His lectionaries, sacramentaries, pamphlets, and hymnals had been thrown back into the bookcase with bindings broken and pages crumpled. The contents of his desk lay scattered throughout the office, as did many files containing personal information about inmates whom he was counseling.

His anger did not come quickly. Little did with Brocard. But it rose from the very core of his being. He felt violated, personally and professionally, and knew that for once he had to take a stand. But against whom and how? He would not act until he had a plan. His years in religious life had taught him that it was never wise to act in the throes of strong emotion.

Interestingly, the only thing not disturbed during the search was the mirror. Despite the frenzied activity that must have accompanied the swag, it was not askew even one centimeter. Curious, Brocard needed to see how it was secured to the wall, to know why it alone had survived the chaos. Placing his hands on either side, he tried to move it on its wire, only to realize it was secured some other way. Until that moment he had never noticed that it lay perfectly flat against the wall. That surely was the reason Custody let it stay in his office. But, rather than settle Brocard's mind, it made him more eager to understand how it had been hung. After a few minutes of fiddling with it—he was never good with his hands—he realized that the heads of four screws imbedded into the cement wall fit perfectly into four holes in the back of the mirror. By lifting the mirror upward on the wall and then out, he was able to remove it. His delight at his discovery was exceeded by what he found next.

Behind the mirror was a large cavity filled with documents and pictures, a cache that might hold the key to what was happening at Brotherly Love. Looking around furtively, hands trembling with nervous excitement, he lifted out one bundle. No sooner had he opened it than he wanted to fold it right up again. The inspector was right: Someone was downloading and printing pornography. No wonder he had to replace his color cartridges so often! Andy had told him they had received a defective order from the new computer supplier. They had chosen the cheapest bid, and they got what they paid for. Or was it Dean who had passed that tidbit of information to him? Brocard noticed he was becoming so stressed that he couldn't remember things accurately. He decided it was best not to jump to conclusions. He rolled up the images of bestiality and abuse and pulled out a smaller roll of papers. Invoices, he discovered. But before he could investigate further, he heard someone coming. He barely had time to replace the mirror.

"Excuse me, Father?" A light-skinned black inmate, someone whom Brocard didn't remember ever seeing before, stood nervously in the hallway just outside his office. "Father, I was at Mass last week. Probably, you don't remember me—I'm Jonathan. They call me the Kid, although I don't like that too much. It's just what they call me, you know."

"Come on in, Jonathan," the priest replied. Brocard was not so agitated himself that he could not recognize worry in others. He was a cleric, after all. And a compassionate one at that, in his quiet way. "Excuse the mess. Let's just clear off one of these chairs, then you sit down and tell me what's on your mind."

"I was just over in the hospital for special meds," Jonathan began once he was seated. "Haven't been sleeping too well for a while—weeks, in fact. Anyway, I was surprised to see your door open and your light on, so I decided to stop by. You don't think I'll get in trouble with my CO, do you?"

"When you leave, I'll call over to the officer on your tier and let him know where you were. Don't worry, you won't get an out-of-place charge."

"Thanks." Jonathan hunched over in his chair and tried to find the words for what he wanted—what he needed—to say. There was a desperation in him with which, this night particularly, Brocard had no difficulty identifying. "I've never been in jail before, Father. This is my first time down, as the guys say here." Brocard wanted to know the boy's crime, but understood this was not the time to ask. Better to just let things tumble out. "I really want to turn things around, Father, but I got into drugs and, well, you've heard all that stuff a million times before."

"Is there anything I can do for you now, Jonathan? Short of listening, that is?"

"It's probably too much to ask, Father." Brocard could see the boy was shaking. "You see, I'm not strong, Father. That's my problem. And I am scared shitless." He paused and looked up. As always, he wondered why people feel they have to speak in a sanitized fashion to a priest. Brocard signaled him to continue. "I'm really scared of some of these guys in here and what they are up to, Father."

"There is not much I can do to help you out there."

"Father, maybe there is. Can I just come down to the chapel during the day when you are here? I can help clean up. I don't have to be paid. My parents put money in my account every month for canteen, so I don't need money. I have to get off the house."

"Any particular inmate you need to avoid?" Brocard could tell that Jonathan was afraid to say the name. So he coaxed it out of him. "I can only help if you trust me."

"Cavallo." Jonathan said it so softly that even God would have had difficulty hearing. "He has used me, and he is so strong and, Father, I really don't want to get into being something I'm not."

Brocard knew Cavallo was capable of forcing himself on anyone, really. But something told him that Jonathan the Kid might not be a hapless child after all. Why had he appeared at just this time? Why did he want to involve himself with the chapel at this time? Was he a pawn belonging to one of the major players in the game of corruption gripping the jail?

As Brocard looked at the boy trembling before him, begging for refuge, he realized that something horrible gripped him as well: paranoia. Unfounded suspicion was beginning to take hold of him. If he allowed it to take control, he would be unable to minister effectively. Fear and hope were incompatible bedfellows.

"Yes, Jonathan," he said after a moment's reflection, "we can find some work for you to do. I'll call you down when I come in tomorrow. Go back now. Rest and try not to worry yourself."

Alone in his office, more uncertain about the future now than he had been when he arrived that night, Brocard decided to go home. There would be time tomorrow to sort through the documents hidden in the wall and to dispose of the pornography. He even resisted the temptation to straighten up his desk. That, too, was a task that could wait.

As he locked the door to his office, he noticed light pouring through the smoked glass doors of the chapel. Someone was inside. They must have entered by the balcony door from the main hallway. Undaunted—it was his chapel after all— he found the key to the chapel doors, opened them, and went inside. As he had suspected, the balcony light was on and someone was rummaging about.

"Hello? Hello, who's there?" he called.

Andy stuck his head over the balcony ledge and, calm as any angel, told him he was sorting through some things because, as he presumed Brocard knew, Maintenance was going to seal off the balcony as of tomorrow.

"I wanted to make sure we had everything out of here we needed."

"Very considerate," Brocard replied. He could not disguise his apprehension. "What exactly brought you here tonight, Andy?"

"The rules are changing, Father Brocard. Custody is going to be all over us in here. Even when you say Mass—you wait. It's a new game now. We have to get ready for it."

Weary from the day, the week, this whole escapade, Brocard told Andy to calm down, to take it easy.

"Can't, Father. Things are moving too fast."

Brocard remarked that he thought things were already moving at lightning speed.

With a cryptic smile, Andy said, "Not by a long shot, Father. Not by a long shot."

Twenty-Eight

Avertanus, my dear old friend,

It is nearly two in the morning and, no, I am not praying my Matins. Would that I were, old friend. No, I am sitting here in the rectory quite alone and more desolate than I've ever been. Even during the bleakest days at San Redempto, when the monastery was quite literally falling down all around us, I cannot remember ever being so devoid of hope. Before you even think it, I want to assure you that I have not despaired—though I am neither a pontifical doctor nor a spiritual director, I know that to lose all hope is the unforgivable sin. Hope does lie buried somewhere deep within me, but at present all I can see around me is unredeemed chaos: a diabolical web of intrigue and suspicion. I have no one to trust, no one even to talk to now that Zinka has returned to Europe. Even her monstrous snoring in the next room would be a consolation at this point. But what I miss most of all—and this has become so clear to me these past weeks—is your sage, kindly presence. Not that you always have your feet firmly on the ground, my scholar friend. Neither of us is very strong in the business of reality, if the truth be known. What you are, though, is honest, and that trumps realism all the time. And you have always listened. Which is why I presume that even here in cyberspace you will not nod off, not cut me short, and never trivialize my anxiety.

Let me go back 48 hours to tell you a few of the things that have concerned me in recent days. I will try to fill in the lacunae in the case of the *Palermo Caravaggio,* the mayhem at Brotherly Love Pen, and my so-called ministry. Perhaps, from your perspective and with your prayerful vision, you will be able to advise me what to do next. That is my hope.

The day before yesterday, Zinka and I decided to go our separate ways. Well, actually, it was Zinka's decision, but I am sure you know that. She said—and I agreed with her fully—that we had to launch a two-pronged attack if we were to get anywhere. She decided I should stay close to the fort, keep my ear to the ground and— well, you get where I am going without my having to strain these metaphors too much. While I keep my eyes open at Brotherly Love, she will attempt to solve the mystery by learning who in the outside world is connected to the criminal activity transpiring behind bars. In pursuit of this, our indomitable professoressa stormed into the office of Professor Mitchum at Bryn Mawr. You no doubt remember him as the art historian she tangled with over the authentication of the painting of Saint Agatha. His academic credentials were as impressive as his morals were dubious. Somehow— neither of us doubts the power of her sexual charms—

Zinka persuaded him to give her the name of a Neapolitan art dealer with Mafia ties. Armed with this, she hopped on the next flight to Paris, where she hoped to persuade her willowy companion Camille to accompany her into the jaws of danger to solve the mystery of the lost *Palermo Caravaggio*. This will surely test their love (and test the effectiveness of Zinka's persuasive tactics with the big boys).

Oh my dear Avertanus, what is happening to me? Just look at those last few sentences. Have I sunk to the level of scripting a grade-B remake of *The FBI Story*? What ever became of the refined language and the delicate sensibility I onetime possessed? Was that, too, an illusion, like so much else around me? Am I being reduced to a cardboard flatfoot, or, worse still, have I returned to my native country after a quarter of a century only to discover how coarse and base I actually am? Rome, my friend, seems increasingly distant. But let me get on with my tale.

That evening I decided to go back to Brotherly Love. What foolishness drew me there at that late hour, I cannot say. Hubris and nothing more, perhaps. In short, I found that Internal Affairs and Custody had taken over. They had seized my computer and searched my office. They found that a considerable amount of pornography had been downloaded on my computer, which disturbed me greatly. It was and still is uncertain whether this was for someone's personal use or to be sold and distributed. As there is nothing private in jail, I am inclined to believe the latter. I was surprised there was no mention of any other information, E-mails, or files regarding the more substantial matters of drugs and art theft. Could that have been removed from the hard drive before the swag? (That is prison-speak for search, excuse me.)

Far more important, the authorities have curtailed my activities in the chapel. The balcony area will be sealed off by a wall, which workers began to construct yesterday. Likewise, an officer will undoubtedly be stationed in the chapel during services. This might be for the best, I know, but all of this makes me doubt everyone and everything around me. Night before last, I found Andy in the balcony as I left. It seems Sergeant Kraus allowed him to organize things there, to take down hymnals and music stored in the organ, so that in the midst of construction activities the next day nothing would be lost. I have no reason to doubt Kraus. Rough as she is, she seems to be a straight shooter. And despite your concerns that Andy might be possessed (and "perfectly possessed" at that), I have seen no signs of dissimulation on his part.

Still, doubt clouds everything I see these days. A poor, distraught, overmedicated inmate came to see me that night. He claimed to reach out for my help because he was being victimized, but I found myself seriously questioning the young man's motives. Am I am so paranoid that I'm no longer effective in my ministry? I wondered. Am I a failure as a priest and as a sleuth?

Today I decided to straighten up my office. I also hoped to talk to Dr. Pouri, the psychologist, whose professional opinion I trusted. But, as things turned out, the good doctor had taken a "mental health day." How fitting. It was also disturbing to see the carpenters throwing up sheetrock in the chapel and blocking off the staircase to the choir loft. Compounding this distraction, officers hovered around as I tried to bring some order to my office.

One important discovery: I located a secret hiding place for documents behind the mirror in my office. I was unable to take a full inventory of its contents. Invoices and pornography, for the most part. I hoped to have time and privacy to inspect these papers, but the day afforded neither. Andy was there, helpful but intrusive, as always. The numerous officers and inmates all seemed more interested in how I was holding up than in counseling or advice.

My hopes of seeing Dr. Pouri were dashed when I received a call from the warden, Tamara Boggs, who summoned me to her office. In her half-educated way, she is a rather daunting lady. However, today I found someone who, like me, is infinitely confused and uncertain about how to proceed. Over and over, she said that rehabilitation, not punishment, was what we had to be about. Private companies cannot see that, cannot allow that to happen, because they are too damn interested in the bottom line. They hire incompetent, burnt-out staff and custody officers because they come cheap. My heart went out to her as she fumbled with charts, searched her memory for ideas that made eminent sense in graduate school but prove to be mere illusions in this environment. She heard the heartless voice of society telling us just lock them up and throw away the key and she felt the hot breath of Custody on her neck. She only hoped I would stand firm. Without you, Father, I have no buffer at all. Custody and Internal Affairs have decided to play hardball, and they don't care who suffers in consequence.

I long for order, my old friend—for those measured days in Rome when we all met in chapel for prayer as dawn broke and when each hour was marked by a familiar ritual. Research into some arcane document, the spaghetti carbonara that greeted us for *cena* on Wednesdays, the singing of vespers each evening. Nostalgia it might be—and I know it was far from perfect— but I simply do not know how much longer I can go on not knowing where I stand and what I am expected to do. Is this, I constantly ask myself, God's work? Or is it not perhaps some horrible distraction from the prayer and good works that I had thought my vocation called me to?

Thank you so much for patiently listening, my old friend. I pray that life in that old-age home in Nijmegen is not getting you down. Do drop me a note when you get a chance.

Your friend, battered but sincere,
Brocard

He pressed "send" and sat looking at the screen for several minutes. He had shared his mind with someone who cared. All his energy drained out of him. The demons were stilled and he sensed that, finally, he could sleep.

Just then his computer announced he had mail. Avertanus, always an early riser, had received his missive. Ever efficient, he sent the following words:

I now have no doubt that the jail in which you minister is evil. My strong advice, as a priest and brother, is that you do not enter that place again until the evil erupts. Let Zinka solve this mystery. Only the ministry of quiet prayer should consume you. I will join you in this prayer, where distance holds no sway and time ceases its inexorable progress. Be still, my friend, and place your trust in Him who is Peace itself.

—Avertanus

Twenty-Nine

WAS THERE A BETTER TIME TO BE A WOMAN than the spring? Zinka, for one, thought not. With the zeal of a convert, she threw herself into searching for fresh outfits, redefining her coiffeur, and choosing just the right scent to announce to all world that Venus had sprung anew from the foam. She sought cuts that flowed when she moved and fabrics that clung tight to her body's dramatic curves. What better place, what better time, than Paris in the spring? Life was a parade: a spectacle of bare thighs, rounded buns, and ample cleavage as far as the eye could see.

The downside was that she had some pressing murders to solve and an organized crime ring to break. But life, especially that of an attractive woman in Paris in the spring, was too precious. One must keep things in perspective. And perspective is what she urged on Camille, her long-suffering companion, as they quit the shops of Les Halles and made their way to the Marais.

"Perspective, my little melon," she cooed over an armload of couture.

"Zinka my dear," Camille said, straining as much to keep up with her as to be heard over the traffic roaring past them on the Rue de Rennes, "Zinka, my dear, think of the risk!"

How Camille had eagerly looked forward to their reunion. She had longed to hear Zinka fumbling with the key in the door—she always arrived unannounced, of course, and at an hour of her own choosing. Immediately Camille would strip naked and throw a Hermès scarf around her neck and wait, supine, for her strong lover to sweep her up and to bring excitement back into her life. There would be ample time to discuss all that had happened in Zinka's full life. (Camille invariably did nothing of note). Then, Zinka slipped into a jet-lag nap from which she would awaken to find Camille worshiping her breasts. Acquiescing to her lover's needs, the weary Slav would abandon herself to the flesh.

True to form, in came Zinka, breathless and oblivious to Camille's naked charms. Words tumbled out of her, expressing her exasperation with Air France and concern whether anything could get done without her. Then she cleaned her teeth, "nothing worse for a girl than stale breath," she always said and proceeded to attack Camille's genitals, as if she were a Tartar plundering a sleepy village. Tongue and hands worked furiously and then, almost as suddenly as it had begun, it was over. In this, Camille always thought Zinka still acted like a man: no romance, no lingering clinch. Naught but the bang in the night.

"Life *is* risk, my timid little girlfriend," Zinka replied. Then, without a word of explanation, she took Camille's hand and pulled her out into six lanes of oncoming traffic. "Hold on tight, we're coming through!" Raising a Prada shopping bag high above her head and flashing the most incandescent of smiles, Zinka marched across the Rue de Rennes with quivering little Camille in tow. Moses crossing the Sea of Reeds could hardly have been more impressive.

"My God, Zinka!" Camille gasped. "What were you thinking?"

"A calculated risk, my tasty bonbon. Nothing more."

"We could have been killed!" Camille was not going to let her get off this time.

"A risk, of course," Zinka soothed. "But these brutish frogs are conditioned to stop to gaze at all things feminine. And after the amount of time and money I've spent on these tits and this ass—" here she lifted and thrust the respective body parts to underscore her point—"I should be able to call myself 'all things feminine,' wouldn't you say?" Seeing that exasperated Camille had no retort, Zinka locked arms with her and strolled towards Beaubourg, explaining her plans as they made their way.

"Now, before we get distracted by frocks, tell me what you have been able to find out on your end from the E-mail addresses I sent you."

"Quite a bit, as things turned out," Camille replied. Away from screeching vehicles, she began to regain her confidence. And, being a research librarian to the core, she could always appear composed when called upon to relay data. "Professor Rosenberg was very helpful in getting me through to the Interpol database. Background information was easy enough to find at our local Internet salon." How the Parisians wallow in all things technological.

"Fine, fine." Zinka was clearly impatient with this professional pedantry. "What you found out is all that is of interest. Not how you got to it, my tedious little turnip."

"The address you gave me is indeed that of Pepe Castellano," Camille continued. "As you suspected, he is the Mafia chief— *capo di camorra,* I believe, is what they call it there—of Naples. Interestingly, it seems the Internet connection is under his grandson's name. His tag, as they call it, is a secondary one. Perhaps this is the reason he took the risk of communicating directly. Keeping clear of direct contact is part of a strict code."

"You mean, he thought he could hide behind his grandson?" Zinka queried.

"More probably, he was playing with his grandson and saw this as an amusing pastime. Castellano's activities are vast—

it seems this little affair with your jail in Pennsylvania is something of a lark."

"Why risk it, then?" Zinka wondered aloud. "What, or more precisely who, is the link?" Camille knew that Zinka's questions were rhetorical; she did her best thinking out loud.

"Although Castellano's empire is far-flung, his lifestyle is, from all reports, very much local and even homey. The villa out of which he works is in Posillipo to the north of Naples, overlooking the bay. But his home is in Vico Equense, the village just outside Sorrento, the traditional seat of the Castellanos since the Spanish occupation."

"No history, dear," Zinka gently warned, "just some facts I can use. Family?"

"A wife who was brain-damaged in a car crash 10 years ago. It seems Castellano himself was the driver, something he rarely did, and since that day has never done again. There is no record of his having sustained any injuries."

"Art. Previous convictions. Details, give me details, my little melon."

"It seems he is a major player in the art market, both legitimate and not. And no, there have been no convictions at all. He pays off the right people and has all informers killed. Very dangerous. Someone to be avoided, Zinka, at all costs."

Then, remembering something she should have done before they left on their shopping spree, Zinka stopped abruptly and, in the most ladylike way she could manage, whimpered a discreet *merde*. Before Camille could learn why she was upset, Zinka asked her whether there were any E-mails in her box from a gallery in Naples.

"*Bien sûr*." Camille had, of course, read it. She pried into all of Zinka's business, which was, for an unabashed exhibitionist like Zinka, one of the things she liked about Camille. "He said he had received Professor Mitchum's recommendation, that he was impressed by your credentials, and that he would be honored to make the requested introductions for you whenever you arrive in Naples."

Barely able to contain her glee, Zinka picked up Camille and swung her about like a rag doll. Both of them let out little squeals, even though Camille had no idea why. They were in the Plaza in front of the Pompidou Center when this happened, and a group of Australian tourists gathered around them, ready to throw coins, caught up in the joy of their moment, whatever it might mean. Two elaborately dressed women ecstatic about spring and each other. Too beautiful to be true, performance art at its best.

Then they stopped twirling and stared probingly into each other's eyes.

"You will come with me to Naples, Camille. You must."

"You are the risk taker, my strong Zinka. I can only wait at home, as usual."

Relieved that she would not have to take Camille with her—she would so get in the way if things turned physical, which she imagined they would—Zinka encouraged her to be brave. Just as soon as they finished their shopping on the Rue des Blancs Manteaux, and had a little lunch on the Place des Vosges, Zinka would be off.

"Don't take too many risks," Camille pleaded. "Please do be careful."

"Risks, my little melon, are what life is about." Then she planted the wettest kiss on her lover's lips, bending her backwards and leaning into her like a veritable Valentino.

At this the Australian tourists could hold back no more. This was better than the fire-eater they had just seen and the man juggling knives just behind them. What absurdity! What passion! They loosed hoots of appreciation.

Coming up for air, Camille, who had truly been lost in the moment, was absolutely mortified. Zinka, on the other hand, saw their senseless adulation as just another sign of the bounty of a spring day in Paris. Extricating herself from her girlfriend, she dropped into the most profound of curtsies.

Thirty

THEY MET IN THE LITTLE BAR OFF THE LOBBY of the Excelsior Hotel, that pile of elegance facing the old port of Santa Lucia. From the beginning, it was plain to see that this was not an equal match. However, Lucio Fidelio, a man so self-involved as to redefine the neurosis, was incapable of seeing it that way. Throughout their time together he was convinced that, sly fox that he was, he always held the upper hand. In fact, Zinka played him like a fine-tuned fiddle. He sang whatever melody she wished to hear.

"*Cameriere,*" he said signaling the waiter with a raised eyebrow, "Campari soda, for me, and the lady would like?"

"Gin, straight up, hold the lime." Elegant as she was—and Zinka had pulled out all the stops from her previous day's shopping spree—she could not bear fussiness when it came to drinks. Probably a holdover from her military days.

"I was impressed by what the good professor had to say about you."

"And what, might I ask, did the good professor"—she tried hard to say those words without smirking—"what exactly did he tell you about me?"

"Cigarette?" Lucio reached one of his reptilian hands into his jacket pocket and pulled out a gold case studded in an array of semiprecious stones.

"Let me be clear about this, Signor Fidelio. If you even try to light up one of those things in my presence, you will regret it. Now, put that silly case away and let's get down to business, shall we? I am hoping to work for Signor Castellano as an archivist. You know him and for a fee, if that is necessary, might be persuaded to introduce us."

Feisty little wench. Exactly the sort of willful creature the Maestro liked to have around. Were he still a masochist—pity no one was these days because he had so enjoyed S/M—he could just see her standing over him with boots and whips, commanding him to do the most degrading of things. Yes, Signor Castellano would be pleased to bring her on board.

Zinka was used to pauses in conversations—lovers often use them for a purpose, as do religious people before particularly portentous pronouncements. But for the life of her she could not understand why this twit couldn't keep a conversation going. From all appearances he was a piece of fluff, a prematurely aging, unbearably affected pawn in the inbred game of contemporary art. Rumor had it that for one brief moment back in the early '70s he was cute. More importantly, he had given his ass to one of the key players in the market: a New York dealer long since gone with AIDS who had bequeathed him his mailing list and a few artists for his stable. That was all he needed to get started. That and the morals of a Caligula, which allowed him to sell himself and whomever he represented to the highest bidder. Although art was his front, Lucio did and would do anything for money. As this was all he knew, he had no doubt that anyone who came into his world was capable of being similarly debased. This was how he looked on the buxom woman before him—

just another body to be bought and sold. Another pawn in the only game he knew, which was, sadly, the only one he thought the world played.

"It is true that Signor Castellano is getting rather old," he said, "and, how can I say it, sensing he will not live forever?" Here the drinks came and Signor Fidelio raised his glass to Zinka.

"Wising up, you mean?" Zinka offered. With a glint in her eye she threw back the gin in one gulp.

"Exactly, as you say, he is gaining in wisdom. When the good professor suggested an inventory be done of Signor Castellano's collection by someone as qualified and well-endowed as you doubtless are, Professoressa, I relayed this to the aging Signor Castellano, and he immediately advised me to invite you to his villa for him to meet you."

"Is that where the collection is, then. Here in Naples?" She tried not to be too direct, but was she going to be given access to the art she needed to see, the hidden works, the black market collection that might hold the *Palermo Caravaggio*?

"Signor Castellano's collection is extensive, Professoressa." Here Lucio propped himself forward in the overstuffed armchair in which, to this moment, his angular and anorexic frame had been all but lost. "Between us, there are many works that have been in his family for years and have lost their provenance." Seeing Zinka was not persuaded, he explained: "The war, Professoressa, and other disasters here in Italy and beyond— earthquakes, floods, Acts of God Himself. The papers, you see, they are gone."

"That is what good Professor Mitchum and Signor Castellano hope I can supply?" She had difficulty controlling herself. A slut she might be, but dishonest: never.

"*Esattamente*. And your recompense would be great, Professoressa." Lucio could see he had her. Evil was so persuasive, especially when it was wrapped in filthy lucre.

"If I were to help you in this—and you must remember I do this at great peril to my professional reputation—I must have complete access to the Castellano collection. Complete and utter access. No holds barred, do you hear me?"

Lucio sat back in his chair, confident he had won the day. "That is up to Signor Castellano, my good professoressa. However, between us," he said, twirling a strand of lank hair in his fingers and licking his pencil-thin lips, "I see no possibility that he could say no to such a tempting offer. Who could, might I ask?"

Thirty-One

Spring had come to Holland, too, but it was a dour, even pestilent affair. Incessant rain had rotted many of the bulbs that had been planted in the garden, causing what flowers there were to be sickly and faint in color. For Avertanus, this was a sign. However hidden, everything was there, if one knew how to look at it with the eyes of wisdom. This sad and inauspicious spring cried out to be heard, like a herald of doom, making crooked the way of the Evil One.

Things were not helped by his daily view down onto the community's cemetery: the place where he too would soon be planted like—if you will permit the metaphor—so many other rotted bulbs that would see no more flowering days. Nor were his spirits at all relieved by the E-mail he had received from his friend Brocard, a dire missive so filled with portents and ill-founded hope as to plunge him into despair. As he could not take it all in on first reading, he had printed out a hard copy so that he could read it again thoughtfully. Which is what he was doing as the rain pelted the windowpane of his monastic cell and obliterated his view of the world outside, where spring ostensibly reigned.

Avertanus, my brother,

She is a wonder-worker, our Zinka. You were so right to advise me to allow her to do what she had to do. Over the past two days, I have received two accounts from her of her activities, and yes, successes, in Naples. Or at least the area of Naples, for she has ventured out into the lair of the fox and, as suspect as her techniques might be, has been able to establish that Signor Castellano is very much the *capo dei capi* of our affair. But I see I am rushing ahead, and I know you well enough to sense your discomfort. So let me start at the beginning, because this is all you are going to hear from me until the end, which I know now is so close that I can hardly bear to be away from my post at the jail. Zinka is doing so much, has already done so much, that I do not want to let her down. But where do I start?

Armed with information that her friend Camille had ferreted out of Interpol documents, information that basically confirmed our suspicions about who Castellano was and what he was up to, Zinka wasted no time in flying off to Naples to meet with the repre- hensible art dealer Professor Mitchum had contacted on her behest. It seems that Castellano needed an art historian of some credibility to fabricate or doctor provenances of several works in his collection, and although the very thought was repugnant to her, she did not disabuse him of the notion that she was his man. So to speak.

The very next day she found herself alone in Vico Equense with Castellano, after having run the gauntlet

of unmarked limousines, machine gun–toting guards at
the gate, and some extremely threatening dogs.
Needless to say, she found the whole process, "delightful beyond belief." Despite her dubious morals, you just
have to love Zinka, don't you? Anyway, there she was
with this old, enfeebled *paesano,* and what do you think
he wanted her to do? Well, perhaps you guessed already:
strip right down to her espadrilles. Again, needless to
say, Zinka had no problem with this whatsoever. In fact,
as she said, it was an uncommonly hot day and she
rather enjoyed the breeze that was blowing off the
Mediterranean and caressing her skin. That was her
word—caressing—not mine. Lest you think I am
becoming too sensuous here in the New World.

As she explained it to me, she had to give a little to
get a lot. So she kept the conversation going as the old
man ogled her, drooling steadily with each layer she
removed. As her top came off, she learned he owned a
series of David sketches of Napoleon, but this was to
be their secret. He was sure she would keep the information between them; otherwise, no telling what
might happen to her beautiful body. As she removed
her panty hose, an effort that invariably delighted her
admirers, he confirmed that many of the works were
not in Italy.

For security, they were in Zurich—"the great
museum of the Bahnhofstrasse," he joked. It was at
that precise moment, as she related the story, that he
caught sight of her clitoris. As the operation left a
large portion of Milorad to create a Zinka, it is a prodigious affair. In fact, the old Don was speechless in front
of it. Then she told him about her favorite artist, the
one for whom she would do anything, anything in the
whole world. He confirmed in a nanosecond that he
himself had a *Caravaggio,* one of his dearest treasures
and greatest secrets.

The other of his great secrets, as it turned, was that in the car accident in which his wife had lost her brains, he had lost his manhood. He was a fallen soldier and, as repugnant as it was for Zinka to see (Why do scarred people love to expose themselves?), she realized immediately that this was a purely "visual rape," as she put it. Something she could deal with quite easily. So for an hour or more they twisted around in the breeze on a balcony overlooking the Bay of Naples, with Capri a heartbeat away. She said the time went rather quickly and the view was quite simply spectacular.

She was also able to learn the extent of Castellano's criminal activities and how they relate to the goings-on at Brotherly Love Pen. Drugs are involved, it seems. She was even offered some pot but, as you well know, Zinka doesn't believe in mixing her hormones with any other substance. From what she could find out, a vast part of his wealth has to do with cigarette smuggling into Italy from Switzerland and Croatia. Her art dealer friend, Lucio, confirmed as much to her. This is what Camille and Interpol had suspected and, as it turns out, what Castellano himself was alluding to when he offered her a cigarette. This is what keeps "papa happy," and this is what will give his "little mama," which is what he began calling Zinka after just one grapple, everything she could possibly want.

But Zinka wants what I want as well: to locate and to save the *Palermo Caravaggio*. Everything else, from drugs to cigarettes, holds no appeal. That alone drives us. And that is the reason Zinka told her randy Mafioso she longed to start work immediately. He said he would accompany her to Zurich and that he had a suite at the Baur au Lac. Although she would have preferred to go alone, she realized it was best to let the old codger have his way. And the Baur au Lac was such a lovely hotel— more great views. How bad could it be?

I told Zinka in my last correspondence that it was no longer possible to E-mail me at my office (not only the modem but the computer itself has been taken away) but that Dr. Pouri, who seems the most trustworthy of the lot, is always online at her little laptop, which she keeps in Front House. That would be the easiest and most reliable place to reach me, as I have decided to go back to Brotherly Love Pen and not to leave until this is resolved. Surely someone will make a move, either to contact Castellano or to clear up the evidence I have already located behind the mirror. I want to be there when it happens. Zinka is doing so much on her end; I just cannot let her down.

Well, my dear, reliable old friend, you see now that things are working themselves out. Pray for me, that I may have the courage to persevere in the work before me. It won't be long now before all of this is behind us and we will laugh again.

—Brocard

Rarely had Father Avertanus, pontifical doctor of spirituality and emeritus professor of mysticism, ever felt so helpless. He could see disaster coming towards his naive but admirable friend. And there was nothing he could do about it.

Thirty-Two

THE ONLY POSITIVE THING THAT PROFESSORESSA ZINKA Pavlic had to say about private jets was that they gave her a sense of privilege. The same could be said of Zurich: a cold city with uninteresting food but devoid of those tiresome reminders of poverty generally to be found in other major cities. Horrid thoughts: jets and Zurich. But for the sake of the *Palermo Caravaggio,* held hostage, she believed, in a vault on the Bahnhofstrasse, she was willing to put up with this and more.

The flight up the coast of Italy and over the Alps to Zurich did offer ample satisfaction for the senses. With the spectacular view out the window to keep her amused and a similarly grand view up Zinka's skirt to titillate Don Castellano, both travelers enjoyed more than enough visual stimulation. The Don's chef prepared an excellent *bracciole* with *pecorino* and *funghi,* accompanied by a full-bodied Montepulciano. Hearty peasant fare, the most treasured food of the Italian *cucina,* done to perfection. The jet was festooned with large clumps of lilac, freshly cut from the bushes that cascaded down the hill of his estate towards the sea, and the scent indulged their noses. Miranna, his housekeeper, had personally cut and arranged the flowers to remind him of the sun-baked *paradiso* he was leaving behind as he ventured forth into the darkness of the north.

Even sound had been considered and supplied in exquisite form. After Zinka mentioned she adored opera, Castellano made sure the tiresome noise of droning engines was softened by a constant array of luscious sounds. Since Renée Fleming, the American diva, was booed off the stage at La Scala during her ill-fated *Macbeth* a few seasons ago, Castellano, like so many of the non-Milanese cognoscenti in Italy, had gravitated to her heterodox interpretations. Her flawless tone filled the cabin, converting and transporting Zinka as well.

She was not prepared for the level of conversation about the arcane world of art that this Mafia don was able to hold. His ear was not just a tool for detecting rumor and plots: He had clearly listened at the feet of knowledgeable scholars. And his eye, roving and perverse as it might be, had spent many hours in study of the technique, content, and style of countless masters. He knew his stuff.

"A paper trail, that is what some of the collection needs. You understand me without doubt, Professoressa?" His formal, proper Italian contrasted shockingly with his meaning. "Somewhere along the way, provenances have gotten lost and with them, perhaps, the all-important authentications. My concern is that they are reconstructed, if lost. And that—how should I say it?—provenances get corrected, if you know what I mean."

She certainly understood what he was asking her to do. With her ready access to archives at the Vatican, the Louvre, and elsewhere, she could alter documents pertaining to works in his collection and plant false papers to establish fictive provenances. She could also expunge "stolen" from a painting's history and insert the name of some untraceable private collector to account for the sale to the don's holding company in Zurich. She was sure the Castellano name would not be found on anything. To implicate him in the theft—her fondest but most far-fetched dream—she was going to have to arrange for him to be caught with forged documents and stolen goods in his sweaty little hands. Not an easy thing to do, but a goal worth working toward diligently.

She moved one step nearer this happy moment the next morning when a director of the Banque Suisse escorted her down into the very bowels of Zwingli's beloved city, the home of the elect. Not four blocks from the hotel where she had left Castellano sipping his morning ristretto, her guide showed her one treasure after another. Then, told not to rush, she was left alone to contemplate the hauntingly beautiful *Palermo Caravaggio*.

Thirty-Three

My dearest little priest,

I do hope you are there, as you need to know all that has happened. Imagine me, Zinka, on edge! But Don Pepe Castellano is in the next room reading Stendhal. Or so he told me: I am not fully convinced of his intellectual pretensions. He is such a randy old man—cannot keep his beady little eyes off me. But let's not go there. If not there, though, where should we go? Descriptions of the luxury in whose lap I sit? Or perhaps the vast trove of masterworks I have uncovered? Or should we just cut to the chase and talk about the *Palermo Caravaggio*?

Excuse my playing you out, as your boys at Brotherly Love Pen might put it, but I had to build up some suspense after all, didn't I? Ever dramatic, your Zinka plays by the only rules she knows. Yes, my little bald pumpkin, I have seen it and will not leave this place until it has been rescued from the grasp of these nasty creatures. It is so sad, sad, sad—I don't even know how to describe it. Excuse my anthropomorphizing, but you know how I do that with paintings I love. They become my children, old and venerable though they might be. And this little baby, this delicate ensemble of deeply pious figures in deep chiaroscuro, has been battered so badly that even time and loving attention might not be enough to save it. I felt not unlike a parent, finally reunited with her kidnapped child, whose joy is constrained by the fact that her little one has been raped and tortured.

Let me tell you what those bastards did. In their ignorance and haste, they cut the painting out of its frame and ripped it off its original stretcher: the only home it had ever known. And if the trauma of this weren't enough, they must have realized it was too large to carry rolled up like a carpet, so they brutally folded it over twice and then, from what I could tell, attempted to roll it as well, presumably to attract minimal attention as they dragged the poor, inconsolable baby through the backstreets of Naples. The resulting damage to the painting is indescribable. The best that can be said for the situation is that Castellano has had a restorer come in to begin the long and tedious process of slowly and carefully restretching the canvas on a rack. Although I know it is for the poor baby's good, this state of the art restoration, replete with computer-sensitized clamps, I cannot help but compare to medieval torture. As for the surface, the cracking, build-up of moisture and loss of paint, it is too early even to begin to think about how to handle that. The hostage lies, huddled in darkness, longing for a good reconstructive surgeon even more than for the light of day.

Sad, too, my distant friend, is the company our *Caravaggio* keeps. Boudin drawings cowering under the shadow of Toulouse-Lautrec paintings— yes, my dearest one, not a poster but a large and impressive oil—and as for supposedly minor baroque church art, the collection is so impressive as to compel one of those seismic reevaluations the art world occasionally undertakes. A Federico Barocci of astounding quality. Not to mention a Salviati that rivals his masterwork in San Giovanni Decollato. But enough. I shake with rage even writing this. And long, as might any mother who has loved a child, to set them free.

This is hardly the place to wonder about Pepe Castellano's moral code. Nor, as I am sure you, my little prelate, would be the first to remind me, am I the one to cast a stone, being far from sinless myself. This is the place to think out loud about what he is up to and about how I can work with him to accomplish the task at hand. When I talked to him about Mitchum and Bryn Mawr, he let slip that he had business connections in Philadelphia. Near enough to begin to think that he, or his organization, might be supplying the contraband flooding into Brotherly Love Pen. He also mentioned several times that he is faithful to anyone who has helped him. That, even were they half-dead or incarcerated, he would never turn his back on them. Does someone at your jail, an officer perhaps, or one of those *banditos* who head up the gangs, have previous contact with him or his organization? Are these things you can find out?

Whatever you can do on your end is, from the way I now see it, icing on the cake. The prize is within my grasp, and whether we catch the culprits on your side of the pond seems insignificant. There is the art historian talking, as you can see my precious little confessor, not someone who longs to weed out evil wherever it may lodge. That is your task.

Silly me, though, to think I can do it alone. Past experience has shown me that we work best, that mysteries get solved and justice carries the day, if we work as a team. Do take care of yourself. I am getting rather dewy-eyed as I write this now. Perhaps the excitement of the day has been too much, but I feel a protective care for you, too, my pious little one. Be careful in that silly, nasty little jail. And do the work you feel you have to do. I will try to get my hands on the *Caravaggio*. Knowing you, a whole other perspective on this will reveal itself—one I need to see.

It is time for me to rejoin Castellano. Such a strange man. On the surface so benign and grandfatherly. He has one of those especially distinguished Italian faces. Not broad and open like mine, but angular, with deep-set eyes and a hairline pushed back to reveal a noble brow. Would that he had used his many talents—physical and probably even mental—to humanity's benefit. His is like the misused talents you have often pointed out to me in the criminal world in which you work. So much beauty and creativity squandered.

He wants to take me out to his *Schloss* on the lake tomorrow. Why he needs yet another home in Zurich when his suite at the Baur au Lac is more than anyone could want, I can't imagine. Then again, my celibate love, profligate wealth in itself is a mystery.

If I do not hear back from you within a day, I will send a copy of this to lovely Dr. Pouri, as you instructed me to do. You must trust her completely before you contemplate including her in our schemes. For the life of me, I do not understand your concern about not being able to contact me. Although danger is still palpable, the prize is at hand.

—Zinka

If Zinka only knew how sadly naive she, for once, had become.

Thirty-Four

SPRING WAS INCAPABLE OF WORKING ITS MAGIC IN JAIL. No matter how riotous the colors might be in the surrounding fields, inside Brotherly Love each season was invariably wrapped in the same drab khaki and brown. As for smell, not even mown patches of new grass in the yard altered the testosterone-drenched stench of unwashed crotch that pervaded every corner. Still, this was Easter time and, even though Brocard was hard pressed to say "alleluia," he knew he had to celebrate Mass and proclaim that redemption was at hand. Sadly, this belief seemed to fly in the face of the reality of Brotherly Love Pen.

No sooner had Brocard passed through the lobby than he succumbed to that siren call of all prisons: routine. Keys rattled and gates slammed behind him with comforting assuredness. Inmates filed past him, keeping to the right, and Custody called out messages to the general population on the intercom, signaling that everything was under control. Chaos, the demon most feared by corrections people, had not yet reared its ugly head. Like everyone else on staff that Sunday morning, Brocard had let down his guard. Not only did he, and all of them for that matter, miss the warning signs. They were also ill-prepared to deal with the crisis when it exploded all around them.

There were more inmates than usual waiting for him to open. Normally, the movement control officer would have sent all of Brocard's workers back to their houses to wait for Mass to be called out. But because of the recent disturbances in the chapel area, an officer had been assigned to stay there throughout the service. It was this officer who allowed inmates like Jesucito, Cavallo, Bear, and several of his *ñetas* to stay.

That this officer was none other than Thomas, the born-again fanatic, was yet another warning sign. From Custody's point of view, he was helping them out, as no other officer had responded to the new posting for "chapel security officer." However, anyone who knew him better understood that his religion was little more than a pious mask for the nefarious activities of a twisted mind.

A third sign that things were not right was how right they seemed. There was little talking in the hallways as inmates made their way to take their doses of special meds, and the atmosphere in the mess hall was practically civilized. Not a fist raised or tray hurled. Anyone who had taken the time to think about it would have realized that something was amiss. But amazingly, no one did. Once the authorities dropped their guard, the scene was set for disaster.

"Father, excuse me, I really have to talk with you," Jonathan said.

"You'll have to wait a few minutes, please," Brocard replied. Why must inmates insist on getting in your face all the time? *A proper finishing school for delinquents—that's what this society needs,* he thought as he fumbled with his keys. Forget the anger management and behavior modification and give these boys some social skills. "After Mass is better."

But Jonathan pushed his way into the office anyway, so desperate was he to have a word with the priest. Problem was, Brocard was not alone. Cuchifrito wanted to know which "songs" they would be singing. (It thoroughly exasperated Brocard that inmates could never call them "hymns.") Jesucito wanted the chapel open so that he and his band of pious felons could pray. Officer Thomas needed to speak to him about how the service— "Mass," like the title "Father," was not in his fundamentalist lexicon—was to be run.

Before anything else, Brocard summoned Beto, his porter, to help set up for Mass. This was a Catholic service, after all, no stripped-down Calvinist affair. Prison or not, he would maintain tradition and perform ritual with proper regard. So, as politely as he could, he told everyone to wait his turn as he opened the cabinets where he kept the chalice, paten, cruets, and lavabo. Also there his alb and the seasonal white chasuble and stole were hung, the hymnals and music stand were stored, and the Easter banners and pascal candle were locked away for safekeeping. As the chief had so prophetically put it when he gave Brocard permission to bring these last liturgical items into the institution: "Jesus, what shanks! You could send 'em out in body bags with those things."

The trick to getting inmates to come to Mass was to have Custody call it out before gym. They were not planners, most of these inmates. They seldom prepared themselves for anything— shops, chapel, classes, even the parole board, on those rare occasions when the board came. A call to chapel was a chance to get out, socialize, see the boys, and maybe—just maybe—to pray.

"Catholic Mass out, large chapel, class-A uniform." For once the announcement was clear. Something was working, at least. Now, as the inmates made their way to the chapel, Brocard finally felt free to turn his attention to the piranha nibbling for a piece of him. But now they were nowhere to be found. Jonathan, red-faced and contrite, was receiving a lecture from Cavallo. It would have been interesting to hear their conversation, but they were just out of earshot. To make matters worse, Cuchifrito was warming up in the chapel. Not that he sounded all that bad—

it was just that he was practicing "Lift High the Cross," which, as everyone knew (from Brocard's perspective, at least) is a Lenten Hymn. Hardly appropriate for Easter time. From the back of the chapel Brocard signaled him to stop, mouthing repeatedly, as if Cuchifrito could really understand: "He's Risen, No Cross."

Then, as Brocard put on his vestments and cast a last appraising glance at the chapel, the last of many signs appeared. Everyone was configured in a most unusual yet completely deliberate way. Jesucito stood apart from everyone, looking desolate, as if considering what he had to do, while his disciples slumbered. The Hispanics—and they were an unusually numerous— banded into small groups, huddled together as if planning how to break through the enemy's defense.

All Father Brocard knew was that the Mass offered comfort. Its measured cadences and unchanged structure were all he could count on in the world of flux to which he was consigned. Raising his hand to signal Cuchifrito to start the opening hymn, he made his way down the aisle, intent on bringing the Peace of Christ to his unruly flock. Sadly, the devil, in the guise of Jesucito or some other equally mundane force of evil, had other plans.

He knew things were not right as soon as the congregation sat and the readings from Scripture began. Armed with his well-worn King James Bible—the infallible Word of God, as he and his brood of vipers were wont to say—Officer Thomas asked the reader to name the exact passage the reading was from. "Acts 4:32–35," the inmates shouted back. Then Thomas stood in the back of the chapel, noisily leafed through pages, and grunted proudly when he found the passage. As if this disruption weren't enough, Jesucito stood bolt upright and raised his arms skyward as he began his own self-satisfied moaning.

Never one for spontaneous emotions, especially in public spaces, Brocard found this behavior nothing short of subversive. Which, of course, it was. However, also not one to easily control difficult social situations, he let Jesucito's affront go as well. Which may have been a critical mistake. Then again, there was probably no stopping the conspirators at that point.

During the responsorial psalm, Jesucito's inarticulate mumblings took shape as words and grew louder.

"The demon is here, and the demon wants to hold on to your mind," he intoned. One after another, inmates began to turn their backs to the altar and to give their attention to Jesucito, as if he were the authority and his word was the Word. Officer Thomas caught Father Brocard's eye and smiled maliciously, knowing he had won. Then, almost inaudibly, after each of Jesucito's disjointed pronouncements, he began to lead the chant: "In the name of Jee-sus."

"And then Jesus, he say crush the head of the demon, crush it now." *In the name of Jee-sus.* "He say you can't find him in worship like this." *In the name of Jee-sus.* "He is in the Word and He is the Word, and the demon he know that." *In the name of Jee-sus.*

The congregation had abandoned the altar and all that Brocard held dear. He did not regret he would not get to preach from the notes crumpled nervously in his hand. But the Church, Eucharist, and the sacrament he had devoted his life to—all of it was under attack. He had to act.

"Thank you, Mr. Perez," Brocard said forcefully. Stunned, Jesucito was momentarily silenced. Then, focusing a maniacal gaze on the priest, he began again. "Thank you, Jesucito," Brocard shouted over his prayers, "there will be a time for intercessions later. Now we have to, we must get on with the Mass. Please," he said turning to the lector, "the Second Reading."

"Disrespect!" a voice cried above the din.

Brocard did not know where the accusation came from—he only knew it was meant to be heard by all. His time in prison ministry had also taught him that "disrespecting someone" was considered the most egregious of offenses, one that never went unpunished.

"The priest disrespected him, man," the voice exclaimed. "Jesucito was just praying. He disrespected him."

Before Brocard could say anything, two groups of about five inmates got up and walked out of the chapel. He recognized them from outside houses, but everything happened too quickly for him to identify the inmates individually. Almost immediately, a dozen or so inmates from the front of the chapel moved toward him. He was more confused than fearful. These were inmates he knew for the most part. Surely they were not going to harm him. Only when he realized they were blocking his path to the red telephone near the sacristy—his only means of contacting Center Control and telling them he needed backup—did he understand what they were doing. As more inmates flooded out of the chapel, the ones who remained became rowdy and downright belligerent. By that time Jesucito appeared less like a preaching Messiah and more like the lone voice crying out in the wilderness. Mass was over long before it had truly begun. And there was no real hope that anyone would go in peace.

"Behold the ravages of sin!" It was Officer Thomas who had taken over now. But his words weren't directed at the remaining inmates, nor were they meant to inspire faith. Thomas meant to condemn one man alone: Father Brocard. "Look at you," he said, pushing his way through the inmates who had encircled Brocard, "dressed up in finery, like the whore of Babylon that you are. This is what comes of your idolatry. Behold the ravages of sin!"

Pulling himself up as far as a very small man is able, and trying not to feel overdressed in his gold-threaded chasuble, Brocard knew logic was not the answer. So, sinking to the level everyone at Brotherly Love Pen, he shouted at Thomas, "Oh, you pompous, silly prick, shut up!"

From what he could tell, it was Bear who started to laugh first: a low rumble of a laugh, almost restrained for someone so large. Then a few other inmates followed suit, until their laughter drowned out poor solitary Jesucito, whose delusional mumblings had once again become incomprehensible gibberish.

"Just shut up and tell me what on earth is going on here," Brocard bellowed. This last command was issued to no one in particular. "I hope to God someone knows, because I sure as hell don't." The priest's unexpected outburst silenced all but a few of the malcontents in the chapel and gave Officer Thomas the opening he needed.

"You don't know anything, do you?" he sneered. "You sad, pathetic little priest." Trying to maintain some composure,

Brocard went over to the president's chair in the sanctuary, sat down and folded his robes as he had been taught in seminary. If he were to be lectured, at least he would maintain some shred of his badly torn dignity.

"Your ways and the ways of the priest before you are over," Thomas fulminated. "We all know it, and it's about time you did too. These inmates come to this chapel because it is their chapel, not yours. They listen to God's messengers, like that Perez over there, and they know what they need to do. You are pissing in the wind here, with your funny outfits and your sad old traditions. You don't see a thing because you are too busy with your empty faith."

"What is it I am supposed to see, Officer?" Brocard countered. "Tell me please, what have I missed?"

"Your way is coming to an end, like the priest before you. It will soon be over."

"Do you know something about Father Norman's death, Officer Thomas? From what you are saying, I am the last to know. If I am to follow him, let me know why."

The inmate circle had broken, although Brocard's passage to the red phone was still blocked. He sensed the inmates were letting the officer speak more out of curiosity than anything else. He knew as well that he was not nervous, that a blessed combination of endorphins and faith was keeping him alert but strangely calm. It was he who was hunting the officer, although no one who witnessed the scene at that time would have described it that way. "Tell me," he prodded the officer, "what is it you know?"

"Things have to get done. It's just the way it is. The other priest, Norman, was killed because he got in the way. He knew about the drugs and the cigarettes, so they got rid of him. But they were working for us, you see, those gangs and inmates who did him in. For the larger plan, God's work and the true Christians. And then that kid, Tony the Faggot who hung it up— we let that happen because he was a prevert."

"*Per*vert," Brocard broke in. "I don't mean to derail your train of thought, and I am certainly not condoning the use of the word, but if he was anything he was a *per*vert not a *pre*vert."

"Anyway, so he had to—to die, you see?" It was clear Officer Thomas had indeed lost his train of thought, just when it was getting interesting. There was something Brocard did have to find out, though. So, taking the lead, he pulled the dimwitted fundamentalist back on track.

"Did you have anything to do with Dean's murder then, Officer Thomas? He was your friend, after all, wasn't he."

"He betrayed the Word. Making money from evil is not evil. But prostituting yourself, lying with another man, that betrays the Word." At this Thomas pulled out his Bible and thumbed furiously for the appropriate damning passage. However, unable to find it and afraid his diatribe might unravel with silence, he forged on. "Yes, I let them get to Dean. Opened the place up, as I did for Tony the Faggot. Thought they were going to have fun, the two of them. God's wrath, praise Jesus, visited them instead. His mighty hand."

"I cannot, for the life of me, imagine why you have confided all this to me, Officer," Brocard observed wryly, "except, perhaps, some misguided belief that I am not going to make it out of here alive to blow the whistle on you. Which I assure you I will, mark my words, I will. It seems equally puzzling to me why you are so homophobic. You have so many opportunities to try things on for size in here. Funny, I never sensed you were gay, but such loathing of others must be rooted in yourself. It is all so terribly sad, Officer. All these deaths and all this hatred, when you might just have had a good time. So where now?"

Officer Thomas was enraged by the accusation. He could never be a "prevert," as he would have it, but he knew that his words alone were not enough to combat Brocard's slander. So, once again, he furiously began to work his way through his Bible, looking for the exact "thus sayeth" passage he needed to show he was equipped with God's mighty armor. However, before he could succeed, Bear stepped forward, still rumbling with a lingering guffaw, to set things straight.

"Thomas, get this right: We used you. No one gives a shit for your silly religion or a shit for you. We throw you a few dollars and you work for us. It was easier for us to make you think you were in control. Little people are easy to deceive that way. You cleared the way for a few nuisances to be knocked off. Period. So shut the hell up, sit down in the corner like a nice little boy, and take your babbling little prophet with you."

"Jesucito?" Thomas cried in disbelief. How easily deflated the self-righteous can be. "You used him, too?"

"*Pendejo*. He was our signal boy, nothing more. Our decoy, get it?"

Just then the main door to the chapel slammed shut, and Brocard realized there was no escape. The real action had moved to other areas, which suited him just fine.

Thirty-Five

IT WOULD BE SOME TIME BEFORE BROCARD KNEW the scope of what was actually happening. As anyone who has been confronted with tragedy can attest, that ignorance was a blessing. If he had thought through matters carefully, he would have realized that, when the trouble first began with Jesucito, small groups of Hispanic inmates had made their way out of the chapel and back to their respective tiers, like commandos on a mission. The last of them closed the fire door to the hallway, effectively sealing off the chapel.

Good monk that he was, Brocard's intuitive response to a fight was flight. In this case—a hermitage on a hill being out of the question—the best he could do was to retreat to his office. Not the most private of places but, given the circumstances, it was the very best he could do. Closing the door behind him, he sat down at his desk and, unable to think of any more effective means of escape, placed his head in his hands. He hoped against all hope that that the blackness that welcomed him was deep enough to block out everything also. He was sadly mistaken yet again.

No sooner had he began to pray than he remembered the mirror. He had to retrieve and hide the papers and photos he had discovered the day before. They might just be the only evidence he had to prove the link between the *Caravaggio* and Brotherly Love. The hallway outside his office was crowded with inmates "pushing up" on Officer Thomas and "getting in each other's faces," as they were so wont to do. He had to hope no one would see him. With the fluid movements of a seasoned *bandido,* he edged toward the mirror, removed it, and looked into the empty hole.

"They're gone. Everything, taken. Don't bother yourself."

Turning around, Brocard saw that Jonathan the Kid, dejected and broken, was seated in Andy's chair. He had been there all along. But, oblivious as ever, Brocard had not noticed. Not knowing what to say, he kept Jonathan in his gaze as he went back to his seat. Better to let the Kid talk, since that is what he wanted to do.

"It wasn't supposed to be like this. None of it." Jonathan heaved a deep sigh and then, more in the style of a soliloquy than a conversation, continued to throw his thoughts into the air. "I was adopted, you know. Always think it's written all over me, but sometimes it comes as a surprise to people. Really rich, my adoptive parents, I mean. Never knew much about my natural parents, except they were maybe black, maybe Thai, maybe Hispanic. Exotic, my new folks always say. A fucking mutt—excuse me, Father, but that's the way it is—a fucking mutt is all I am."

Brocard had no desire to fill in the pauses. Above all, he had no desire to turn this into a counseling session. His chapel was under siege, he had effectively lost control, and he saw that someone had removed the telephone jack, making it impossible for him to call for help. The red phone in the chapel, his only other line to reach the outside world, was out of his reach. No, now was the not the time to console, but rather to panic. He looked at Jonathan with impatience, trusting the young man would come to his senses and get to the point.

"You probably want to know what's happening, what I know about it. Well, not a whole lot, I guess, but a heck of a lot more than that asshole Thomas." The Kid sat back in the chair and spread his legs wide, the way men do when they want to show they are in control of something. And, just in case Brocard missed the body language, he rubbed his crotch a few times. Unfortunately, he sneezed as he was doing this—a high pitched wimpy little wheeze of a thing—which irretrievably wrecked his pose.

"Everyone knew about that stash behind the mirror. No big secret. Just part of the activity. The gangs, some officers, your guy Andy—he's a big part of it, maybe even the kingpin. Don't know how high up it goes, but they are all in it together. Everyone but you. All I get out of it is being screwed by Cavallo. Which I said I hate so that I could get into your office in case your clerk got found out. Sorry, father, they told me to do it." Brocard did not drop his eyes, confident that if he gave the Kid the attention he so desperately wanted, he might get the information he needed in return.

"Oh, yeah," the Kid continued. He could not stop talking now that someone was listening to him, "I hated it at first. Getting fucked like a woman and all. That monster thing of his ripping me apart. But then I decided just to let it happen. Everyone does it with Cavallo—there's no saying 'no' to him. Starting to enjoy it, really. You know, now I even ask him just to spit on it before he shoves it in. No KY or anything. Just spit, you know."

Enough was enough. This information Brocard could easily live without. Fortunately, the situation changed abruptly. The door to his office flew open, and Bear, appearing larger than life in the narrow doorway, told Jonathan in an almost fatherly tone to leave. He had to talk to the priest.

"Everything is going down," Bear said. "I wanted you to know you will not be hurt. You are our priest. We're going to use you but not hurt you. Get that?"

"Well, not exactly," Brocard replied. He tried not to be too professorial—he knew his pedantry exasperated absolutely everyone—but still he needed some clarification. "Please," he offered Bear a seat, more from a desire not to have the giant looming over him than from a concern for Bear's comfort. When he saw that Bear had no interest in easing into conversation, he asked the main question as directly as possible.

"So, Bear, what the hell is up?"

Smiling to hear his priest talk real talk but intent on getting down to business, Bear closed the door behind him and, in a manner as terse as the Kid's was florid, told Brocard the who, what, where, and how.

"Padre, you see we have to look out for ourselves, so we do these things."

"The *ñetas*?" Brocard wondered. "What is it you have to do, then?" He didn't want to interrupt, but he needed to get things straight.

"You see, Padre, no one looks out for us so we have to do for ourselves. There is this thing we've got here. This thing with cigarettes and hooch and drugs."

"And art?" Brocard ventured. Hard as it was to imagine someone so unsophisticated having anything to do with his blessed *Caravaggio,* he had to find out. "Paintings, too, Bear? Art?"

"We got some of that stuff too. Anything that sells. We have connections out there." Bear seemed less sure of himself on this topic than he did when he took credit for the more conventional prison activities. Still, the question about art did not set him back; he clearly knew something about the *Palermo Caravaggio.* How much was hard to say.

"We use people, Padre, because we have to. No other choice in here. *Pendejo* Jesucito, he was an easy one. Thinks he is a *profeta.* Some sort of holy man. It was easy to get those black people annoyed at the chapel when they thought he was being 'disrespected.' They're really into that, you know: talking about disrespect. Don't know what it means, people like that. We used Jesucito as a diversion. That's what you Anglos say, right? He was a diversion and also our signal boy. Today when he went, our commanders went off to their posts. To start things up."

As Bear talked, Brocard noticed that Andy was standing motionless at the office window. If he wanted to come in, he did not say. If he felt anything, it was impossible to know what. There was a strange strength to him—a diabolical composure.

Sensing someone was there, Bear looked over his shoulder and saw Andy, just inches away but still out of earshot. Turning back to Brocard, he momentarily suspended his plan to tell the priest what had precipitated his gang's eruption and how far it was to escalate. Instead, he said a few words about Andy, the faithful clerk.

"He's one of us, you know."

"How can a white boy be a *ñeta*?" Brocard queried. "I thought you had to be Hispanic to get into—"

"A front. We have these white boys who do our work. And your good boy Andy, he was the best. Worked that computer for us, placed orders. Did everything like a good little Anglo slave." Bear turned to flash Andy a smile, the kind that pimps give to their whores. For his part, Andy stared blankly ahead, looking more like an automaton than flesh and blood.

"So we had this great thing going, and then we get a few little setbacks. You were one of them, with your snooping around the computer and all. But the worst one of all is that bitch in Front House."

Brocard had to think for a moment to figure out whom Bear meant. Administration was so far removed from his daily life, as it was from the lives of inmates, that it took him a second to figure out that the bitch out front was the warden, Tamara Boggs.

"It all started when she tried to move in on STGs, that's what they call us: security threat groups." Bear virtually spat out the words, showing something of the anger that was boiling just beneath the surface. "First, they started setting up cameras everywhere. Then they started to 'validate' people who made hand signs. You know all that crap that's happening. Made it harder and harder to get our work done. But not impossible. We were able to get on with things pretty good. Until now that is."

"What changed things, Bear?" Brocard asked gently. As

annoying as this whole charade was, he leaned on his pastoral skills and affected a concern that would have taken in anyone.

"We got information—we have our sources you know—we got information that the black woman was targeting Hispanics. Not the Bloods, her people, but us. We have to get her out, and what better way than to show she has lost control? When she's out, we get back in power again. This time, no one will stop us."

"Excuse my acting as the devil's advocate here, Bear," Brocard interjected. Clearly the phrase meant nothing whatsoever to Bear, so the priest shifted gears. "When the authorities find out that an Hispanic gang started an uprising, won't they be even more controlling? With or without Warden Boggs?"

"Now that's the beauty of this thing," Bear replied with a broad smile. "Because they are not going to find out, are they? With white boy Andy as our front, and you as his shield, the Commissioner isn't going to hear anything but Anglo noises. And Anglo reasons why this has happened. You know, bad living conditions and all that shit. Your boy Andy has the list, he knows what to say."

"And what is to say that I will not let people know the truth? This isn't confession, you know?" Even if it were, Brocard thought, intent to do bodily harm was not privileged information, and he would have no qualms about telling the authorities the true story.

"No, we wouldn't hurt a priest, you're right. If you did, Padre, we would get that sister of yours on Roberts Road in Bryn Mawr. Bang her up and knock her down."

Until that moment, Brocard had never considered the risk his bizarre ministry might pose for his family. Yes, he would keep quiet. Both he and Bear knew he had to.

"Now, get up slowly and follow me, Padre. We have work to do."

Feeling smaller and more insignificant by the minute, Brocard went over to Bear, who signaled for him to turn around. Bear forcibly pulled Brocard's arms behind his back and escorted him out into the hallway. Looking into the chapel, Brocard caught sight of Officer Thomas, bound and trussed like a turkey waiting to be roasted, trembling in the back pew. Were it not Officer Thomas, who in truth needed a little humbling, he might have felt compassion. As it was, he was more concerned with his own fate. Especially when the Pascal candlestand, a massive piece of metal, came hurtling towards him.

As things turned out, the projectile flew right past him and into Andy's waiting hand. Quite athletic, Brocard thought. Then, armed with his holy lance, Andy took Brocard as his shield and slowly made his way to the door to the main corridor. Jeering inmates flanked their path.

Once out in the hall, Brocard caught the stench of smoke, which seemed to be coming from all directions. Try as he might, he could not keep himself from shaking. He wanted so much to be strong, but something within him succumbed to fear.

"Father," Andy said as he pulled Brocard toward him and drew as close to the priest's ear as his conscience. "Chaos will win, as it always does." Then, rumbling with a laugh that belonged to the devil himself, he said, "You don't know shit, Father. You don't know shit."

Thirty-Six

"NOTHING STUPID, YES, I PROMISE," the warden said. Nothing could have prepared her for this moment. Certainly no graduate seminars or weekend workshops—the training she relied on and boasted about so often. "I will be in my office shortly, Lieutenant. No rash move will be taken. Nothing until I hear further from you, you have my word." Putting down the receiver, Tamara Boggs tried to decide what to do first.

Well, the super-tight little shorts had to go. She had a nice butt, which the dignity of her position as warden required she keep concealed. Except on days off, which this was supposed to have been. Her first executive decision was to don the nearest sensible pantsuit her nervous hands could find. Then she had to call the local police, to alert them to the riot. The chief would have to be pried away from his easy chair, of course. He could contact the state authorities as she made her way back to the office to await instructions. "Instructions": the very word made her head spin. The indignity of it all: instructions from inmates. In her jail. On her watch.

Although the warden's house was only a two-minute ride from Front House—the Administrative Offices at Brotherly Love—Tamara had ample time to replay the conversation with the lieutenant at Center Control her mind to come to terms with what had taken place. If coming to terms with anarchy was even possible.

Her phone rang. "Hello, Warden. Lieutenant Childress here. First shift, Center Control. Yes, the one who's a bit slow, yes, Ma'am. Warden, we've got ourselves a situation here. I can only say what they want me to because they have a gun pointed at my head."

"Whose gun might that be, Lieutenant?" the warden asked calmly. She knew this was not the time to be snide, but she had a lot of snide in her, and it just had to get out.

"Well, mine, Warden." Then, realizing this was open to misinterpretation, the lieutenant added, "mine before they took it from me and pointed it at my head."

Before Tamara had a chance to come out with any wisecracks or give him any attitude at all—the last thing in the world any hostage needs—the lieutenant began reading the prepared speech. Cavallo had given it to him shortly after making his way into Center Control under the pretext of fixing their sink. Quicker than you can say "plunger," he had overpowered the lone civilian stationed there as well as Lieutenant Childress, a man whose brain was dwarfed by his gun. In a time of cutbacks, it was deemed unnecessary to overstaff Center Control. But what personnel remained barely constituted a staff at all. And they were definitely no match for Cavallo with a wrench.

"So here's what they say I have to tell you, Warden. Listen up now, all right? Here goes." Lieutenant Childress cleared his throat, rustled the paper, then read the prepared inmate demands:

"'We, the inmates of Brotherly Love Pen, are fed up with a whole lot of things. We got our rights and they are being disrespected. So this is what's happening. We took over the jail. That's right, the whole thing, from Center Control to Big Yard and everything in between.'"

Tamara tried to consider how this was possible. But, not being an inmate, she couldn't see how easy it had been. Were she one, she would have realized that anything was possible on weekend mornings, with movement and Custody's guard down. officers regularly left the cell doors open around midmorning as they waited for inmates to return from canteen, the gym, or, for the pious few, Mass in the chapel. With only one officer on each house, it was easy for a group of inmates to overpower them. The only major problems were the control booths.

The movement post, which controlled the gates between the prison complex and the outside houses, was staffed by Officer Bivings. She was so easy to play out. Being lazy, she let the gates stay open during movement. And, thinking herself invulnerable, she always came right over to the opening in the bars to talk to any inmate who wanted to share something with her about Jesus. Just hold up your Bible with your finger on a verse and she was there. How easy it was to grab her neck and threaten her with death if she didn't turn over the keys. Which, praise Jesus, she did in a flash. Leaving only Center Control—the easy prey of Cavallo and his trusty plumbing tools—to fall.

"'The food sucks. The visit schedule is no good for most of our women and children to come, now that you don't allow visitation on Sunday so you can save money. And what about this money thing? We haven't gotten paid for two months because of this computer-is-down thing. Nothing is ever in canteen anyway, no chewing tobacco or no octopus anymore. What is this? Don't you guys pay your bills? On top of everything, we are fed up with our calculation sheets. Can't you guys figure out the difference between a flat term and a stip? Need some help from us? We sure as hell want you to do your work. When we get these demands met and a promise from you that there will be no reprisals, then we will release the guards and give you your jail back.

"One final thing: No fooling around. No storming the place or anything like that, or a lot of people will pay. Your people, with your guns, which we have. Be in your office soon with an answer.'"

As she fumbled with her keys to get into her office, Tamara Boggs was thankful that, so far no lives had been lost. No real damage had been done. As for the demands, they were pathetically too simple. *What,* she wondered, *is really happening here?* Inefficient and arrogant as she might be, the warden was no one's fool.

Meanwhile, Cavallo opened the gate for Andy, who still had Brocard in tow. Before entering Center Control, he looked down both corridors to see that everything was clear, not only for him but for Bear and the remaining inmates in the chapel. A few stayed to make sure Officer Thomas went nowhere and that no one tried to get in through the skylights on the roof. A couple of inmates fought for the right to stand sentry with the officer's revolver. The others, with Bear in the lead, broke off into small bands and charged back to their tiers, like reinforcements come to turn the tide of war.

"Sit down and shut up!" Andy commanded. Although his behavior was brusque, Brocard began to suspect that his demeanor was an act, a part for which Andy was ill-suited. But, not wanting to tempt fate, the priest held his tongue.

"We fucking did it. Fucking did it, man!" Andy exclaimed as he pulled Cavallo toward him and kissed him on the lips, so long and so passionately that even the lieutenant, slow as he was, started fidgeting nervously. It was Cavallo who came up for air first, but he was not the first to speak. For Andy, this was his moment of triumph and he was bursting to tell Brocard, his old boss, about it. Nothing to lose now, he thought. And how very gratifying to rub the priest's nose in his own shit. What could be better than that?

"What idiots you all are!" he screamed. "So easy to play out and so easy to destroy." Putting down the Pascal candle lance— the guards were bound and Cavallo had the pistol, so he had nothing to fear—Andy began to strut around Center Control like a peacock. "You're no match for the devil, you know. That's who

I am, if you didn't know. He's in me and makes me destroy things. Just the thought of that was enough to scare the first priest to death. Idiot priest. He tried the holy water and name of Jesus stuff on me, and when I laughed in his face—poof, he foamed at the mouth and he was gone. Just like that. I didn't always know I had the devil in me. Have Cavallo here to thank for that. When I realized I did, I knew I could do anything. Control those gangs with information. Get my hands on art and dope. There was no stopping me. People believe me, you see. You believed me and you still don't see what's happening, do you? Do you?"

What Brocard saw, but couldn't report because he was too horrified to speak, was that Cavallo had come up behind Andy and was pointing the gun at his head.

"The honest-to-God idiot here is you," Andy ranted. "The devil? You'd eat any shit I fed you."

Thirty-Seven

GOD, HOW THEY HAD LONGED FOR THIS MOMENT. They were sealing the perimeter of Brotherly Love Pen and flooding into the warden's office, EMTs and a SWAT team, not to mention the Federal Emergency Evaluation Team, better known as FEET. It had been a long time since any of them had seen real action; many, in fact, had only experienced the feeble joys of those simulated disasters staged in the parking lot of the Blue Balls Marriott. Now, the men and women of the entire alphabet soup of emergency preparedness could not contain their glee that the real thing had finally arrived.

Mercifully for Tamara Boggs, Dr. Pouri had arrived as well. Her professional skills and feminine composure were just the tonic the warden needed to keep from breaking down, something she had never thought herself susceptible to before the sky fell.

"Doctor, may I have a word with you," she asked in a quavering voice. From the desperation in the warden's eyes, Kris knew this was less a request than a cry for help. "Oh, sister," Tamara continued in a whisper, "I am so scared. They are going to ask me what to do and I won't know what to say to them. I can't think of anything to say."

"There is nothing to say right now," the doctor soothed. She had turned into Kris, a girlfriend Tamara could trust. The transformation suited both of them perfectly. "Look at all of these mindless brutes puffed up and swaggering about. Is that what you want to be, Tamara?"

"Hell, yes," the warden said with a bitter laugh. "What dyke worth her salt wouldn't?" Kris observed that the stress of the situation had broken down the warden's normal defensive secrecy. Career-obsessed as Tamara was, that this might be a come-on never crossed the psychologist's mind. "Nothing would suit me better than slathering on a fistful of that topical testosterone, strapping on a dildo and pulling out the assault rifle." They could not help smiling together at the image Tamara had conjured. The moment faded quickly when the office telephone rang. As Tamara picked it up she knew, as surely as the emergency honchos hovering around her, that the moment of truth had arrived. She had to make decisions and take action.

"Jesus. Is that you, Father Brocard?" Without waiting for an answer, she added, "I hope to God they haven't hurt you."

"No, I am quite alright." Brocard's voice was weak and uncertain. Things were clearly not right with him. "Warden, I have been asked, told, I guess is more appropriate, to pass on a series of demands from the inmates. First, they want me to tell you that all guard posts have been secured and all tiers taken over. Custody has no control at all any more." His voice cracked as he was saying this, then the phone went briefly silent as he received new instructions from Cavallo.

At this point FEET took over. Clumsy as their name, they had hooked up some ridiculous contraption to the warden's telephone. It was supposed to pick up and enhance background sounds so that inmates' voices could be recorded and identified when the nightmare ended.

"Tactical fires have been set and—" Brocard began, before the warden interjected.

"Back up, Father. What are we talking about here? What is a tactical fire?"

Brocard himself was not sure what this meant. Covering the mouthpiece a second time, he got something like an answer from Cavallo.

"All they will say is that these fires are to get you to decide quickly to meet their demands. These fires, they tell me, are controlled. But if action isn't taken soon, they won't be."

If Tamara had looked over to her door she would have noticed that a lieutenant was speaking to one of the FEET officers about just this matter. The police helicopters had noticed smoke coming from several of the houses. Wispy though it might be, there was no telling how the fires might behave if they got into the ducts and wiring. But the lieutenant had to wait his turn to speak with the warden, who had more than enough to worry about.

"You have my word," she said. "Tell them they have my word, Father. No assault, no rash action on our part. Amnesty to all inmates, unless—and you make sure you tell them this—unless they harm any staff or officer. I will get back to you within the hour on all of the other demands. The food packages, contact visits, restoring the weights to the gym, everything. Just let me get it sorted out with the Commissioner. Tell them, please."

Having received the answer he wanted, Cavallo signaled for Father Brocard to hang up. Knowing he had only one chance to find out what really was happening, Brocard asked whether Dr. Pouri was there. At this point, nothing would have surprised Tamara Boggs. Without a second thought she handed the phone to the psychologist.

"Doctor," Brocard said with increased urgency, "I just wanted to find out if everyone is OK." The FEET surveillance team and assorted inmates who heard his question thought he was showing pastoral concern. Nothing could have been further from the truth. And Kris Pouri, who had longed to be a sleuth since their first meeting, instantly knew she had finally arrived.

Now, how to tell Brocard she had heard from Zinka? She had to think fast.

"Sex, if you excuse my saying, Father, is the most potent force at work. It cuts through everything and is even controlling the Christ Child." Too vague, perhaps? Was the pause on his end bafflement? Or did he read Zinka for "sex" and the *Palermo Caravaggio* for "the Christ Child," as she hoped? When he spoke next, she had to presume he understood, because his question was so totally unrelated.

"Is there any inmate that I should be particularly solicitous to?" the priest asked. "Anyone you feel I should have special *pastoral* concern for?" Although Brocard stressed the word 'pastoral,' she knew quite well what he meant.

"Not your clerk, he need not concern you. There might be another, but I have to look into the records because I get confused with names sometimes. Too many aliases."

Brocard was relieved that Zinka had abandoned her suspicions about Andy. If only Andy had known this earlier, he might have been spared a gun to his head and intense embarrassment. Seeing that Cavallo was loosing patience with his extended call, Brocard said goodbye to his friend the good Doctor with one last courageous line.

"Kris, go riding. I know how horses make everything come together for you."

At that the telephone went dead and so, too, did the atmosphere in the warden's office. Everyone—Tamara, FEET, the lieutenant at the door—struggled to figure out what on earth was happening. They were sure of one thing only: Father had lost it. Brocard, on the other hand, could only hope that Dr. Pouri had understood the message about Cavallo in his final words to her. If so, he believed, Front House might realize how limited in scope this apparently prison-wide takeover actually was.

"The demands are reasonable," Tamara said, breaking the silence. "Changes have been made too quickly around here, without considering any consequences except the bottom line." Then, sitting back in her chair, she began to share with Kris her worst fears.

"How horrible it would be if this place became a typical jail. If we can't try to help these men, change at least some of them, then this is not a job I want." Tamara Boggs had a vision, and enough talent to make it a reality, in another place perhaps (not a privatized cash-cow) and in another time (not during a prison takeover). In fact, no one was listening to her at all. Her friend Kris ran out the door, excitedly saying something about checking out a horse. FEET men played back the tape of Brocard's voice. And the lieutenant began to scream into his walkie-talkie.

"Not the whole fucking thing? Going up in smoke? Come in! Come in!"

Thirty-Eight

HER TITS WEREN'T HALF BAD, REALLY. MAYBE IT was the fact that it had been far too long since she had played with them, or maybe it was simply that Zinka missed her girlfriend's clever little mouth roaming freely all over her body. Whatever the case, she was happy to see her lover driving through the gates of Castellano's villa on Lake Zurich. And happier still—lust aside— to hear the progress Camille had made on the case. It was wonderful to have a cute, absolutely brilliant, and tirelessly dedicated girlfriend. In a word, happiness was Camille.

"Don't 'my little melon' me!" Even when she tried hard, Camille simply could not do stern. It simply wasn't in her nature. Still, given the silence on Zinka's end for so many days and her seeming lack of concern, she had to give it a try.

"Do shut up and let me hold you," Zinka cajoled. "Don't you see, my adorable pet, I couldn't call you. I absolutely couldn't risk anyone thinking that there was more to my interest in Castellano than his art and his sick little sexual games."

Camille pulled back and gave Zinka one of the petulant hurt-little-girl looks she did so well. Sighing, Zinka assured her: "No fingers shoved up my brand-new slit could ever reach my heart." Not the most soothing words for someone of a jealous nature, but the most apt the ever-earthy Zinka could offer.

For the life of her, she could not understand Camille's little moods, which were often triggered by the smallest of her comments. In her desire to understand—Zinka did love Camille, after all, and was intent on making their relationship work—she attributed them to a lifetime soaked in estrogen, as opposed to a plunge taken in midlife. This theory worked far better for her than the idea that she might be a brutish boor.

"Now do sit with me over here on this splendid Louis XVI chaise longue," Zinka gently commanded. Ever the professoressa, she felt it important to inform Camille of the quality, and undeniable authenticity of the objects that crowded the room—and indeed, the entire villa. "Let it be noted," she added with a broad smile, "crime definitely has its rewards."

Then, lowering their voices like the conspirators they were, they exchanged the information each had gathered. Zinka's main interest was to find out about Castellano's activities in the States. In this Camille did not disappoint. Interpol, together with the FBI, had confirmed that he had made two trips to the Philadelphia area within the last few years, the most recent in the spring of 2000. It was not possible to get a list of all of his contacts—if such a list existed—but the dates alone allowed Zinka to disqualify Andy and Dean, two of her prime suspects. At that time both of them were incarcerated.

"How, my moist little plum, were you able to get the big boys to give you this information?" Camille was still not comfortable with Zinka's detective-speak, but she let it pass. The inducement, she explained, was the *Palermo Caravaggio*. They knew all about it, and had suspected Castellano for years, but could never pin anything on him. They even knew that the painting and numerous other artworks were stored in a bank vault on the

Bahnhofstrasse, which Interpol types referred to as the world's greatest museum. But, given Swiss privacy laws, the authorities had little hope of retrieving the precious loot. Until Zinka and Camille came along.

"So they are willing to play, are they?" Zinka asked.

Pursing her lips and acting unusually coy, Camille pushed herself away from Zinka and slowly moved to the door. Opening it, she signaled for the man waiting outside to join them.

"Professoressa Pavlic," she said rather formally, "allow me to introduce you to my husband." Then, with an elaborate flourish, "Henri Blanchierdarie."

It was now Zinka's turn to affect jealousy, short-lived though it might be. She had no fear that Camille, a sister to the core, would ever fall for someone of that other sex. And she had no doubt this supposed husband of hers was anything but an Interpol operative.

"A pleasure to meet you," Zinka said, laying on the charm. "I did, of course, see someone of the masculine persuasion drive up with our little Camille, but I presumed it was merely a chauffeur. How clever of you to be an intimate." Blanchierdarie, whose real name was Henry (Harry actually, but that's a whole other story) had no idea what Zinka was talking about. Not being a lesbian by a long shot, he was oblivious to the internal dynamics of the relationship into which he had stumbled. In any event, he had one job and one job only: to retrieve the *Palermo Caravaggio*. And to this end he was willing to endure even the most tortuous confusion.

Henry—a.k.a. Henri—clicked his heels and took the professoressa's hand to kiss it. A keen observer would have noted a momentary pause as he marveled at the size of Zinka's paw, but since everything about the situation was awkward, none of the players gave it a thought. Trying her best to be ladylike, Zinka held her tongue, since Henry obviously wanted to speak first.

"Excuse my barging in as well. I have already seen our host, Signor Castellano, and told him that since Camille's career as a researcher and mine as an genetic engineer seldom allow us to get away, I seized the opportunity to spend a few days on the lake with her. I've brought work with me and will not get in the way."

"Henri is such a dear," Camille said taking his hand in hers and, rather convincingly, resting her head on his shoulder. "He folds up into the smallest of spaces."

"I bet he does," Zinka said as she pulled herself up to show him she was no one to trifle with. Professionalism aside, the green-eyed monster was rearing its ugly head. "And you, you man you, you expect to stay here in a room with Camille, do you?"

"I wouldn't have it any other way," a voice came from behind. They all turned to see Signor Castellano, rather distinguished in his uniquely gnarled way, hobbling into the room. He was flanked by a couple of overdressed lackeys. "You, my professoressa, need your researcher. She has her needs as well." Then, in a display of machismo that bordered on the ludicrous, he groped himself and said lasciviously: "We all have needs which must—which will—be met."

Thirty-Nine

THE GREEKS DID TWO THINGS EXQUISITELY WELL: sex and tragedy. Wisely, they often saw the two as inexorably linked—a truth to which anyone who has lived life fully can readily attest. As things heated up at Brotherly Love and as the story of the *Palermo Caravaggio* drew to an end, hubris, the downfall of any classical hero, was evident on all fronts. Overarching pride and feelings of invulnerability were everywhere. This, coupled with unbridled sexuality, was a sure recipe for disaster.

Hubris had infected Prison World Inc. a long time ago. Fully confident they could endlessly pad the bottom line while skimping on security and essential services, the company's directors believed they had discovered the alchemist's trick for turning society's shit into gold. For them, a correctional institution was little more than an inner city Boys Club. Just give the inmates an old basketball with a bit of bounce left in it and let them tire themselves out. Like the misers who ran so many other private prison companies, their pride and greed made them put the lives of the incarcerated and their keepers at risk for the sake of money.

It was hubris, too, that filled Chief Janochek as he puffed around the warden's office, trying to persuade the world and himself that he alone knew how to quell the uprising. "Hell, I've seen worse than this in my day," he averred. He hadn't, of course, but no one was listening to him, except when he gave one unfortunate command. He believed inmates might try to escape from the Outside Houses. To avert this, the chief ordered the perimeter tightened. To shut him up, the warden agreed. And as they were too busy with hostage negotiations and their high-tech toys, both Internal Affairs and FEET paid him no mind, to their eventual dismay. As the chief paraded around, confident he had won the day, pride heralded his downfall—and lost them their man.

Egomania was endemic to the two inmate factions involved in the Brotherly Love takeover. Each was determined to win the day and loathe to share information with the other. Because neither group saw the big picture, neither gained the upper hand.

For Internal Affairs, this was gang activity, pure and simple. And on that, they had done their homework. They had profiles of Bear and all his *ñetas*, charts of probable weapons they might use for slashing throats, their preferred method of intimidation, but no clear plan for how to combat them, short of locking them in their cells. For their part, FEET was prepared to storm and invade, without having the slightest clue what or whom they would find at the other side of the gates. Of course, this all played into the hands of the felons, but they too were divided— by greed, ignorance, and delusion.

Warden Tamara Boggs staged her own tragedy within the larger, sadder tale. It didn't have to be so. She might have been the heroine she had always aspired to be if she had only allowed others to help her. Even a big-city dyke can't go it alone. If she had only been forthcoming with Kris Pouri, the doctor would surely have told her of the progress Zinka Pavlic was making in Zurich. With the big picture in view, she would have understood the real reason chaos had come swaggering into her jail. Then she could have taken the appropriate steps. As it was, she remained in a snit, confident that, since Kris Pouri had run out on her, she didn't need the doctor or anyone else, for that matter. Her silly pride led to her sillier fall.

But perhaps the most intractable hubris was Andy's. There he was, his supposed lover pointing a loaded revolver to his head, his hands bound by a reluctant Father Brocard, as acrid smoke filled the custody station where they had been led. Despite the fact that Cavallo and his crew were on a rampage, Andy simply knew with his whole being that he had nothing to fear. Because he believed he—and he alone—was in control." See that hatch down there?" Cavallo sneered at Brocard. "Hey, priest, I'm talking to you. That hatch over there in the floor behind the lieutenant's chair? Now open it, pull the door all the way back, that's a good little priesty. Now slowly—don't go too fast, or I'll have to waste bullets on you and that won't make me happy—slowly go down the stairs and wait at the bottom."

This was the most Brocard had ever heard Cavallo speak. Granted, they weren't the most eloquent of words. Nevertheless, they did indicate a forceful, not to say loquacious, side of Cavallo's personality, which Brocard could not have imagined. Fortunately, he was a well-trained monk who was used to obeying orders blindly. He opened the hatch, lowered himself into the tunnels, and waited patiently for the next order.

For his part, Andy had no doubt that once Cavallo had disposed of the priest and they were out of sight of the officers, the ruse would be over. He could hardly keep from smiling now that success was within reach. But, of course, it wasn't.

"Get that smirk off your face," Cavallo growled. It was clear he meant what he said. Andy finally understood that the tables had been firmly turned. "You just don't get it, do you? Walk slowly, the two of you. I'll tell you where to turn and when to stop."

As Brocard and Andy made their way through the tunnel, they had to wonder where they were being taken. And why. If Cavallo wanted to escape, why would he need them? Curiously, neither captive was truly concerned for his life. Despite the hardboiled role Cavallo was playing so well, both of them had known him as a brainless sex machine for so long that, try as they might, they could not see him in any other light. About this, they were right.

"Why, Cavallo?" Brocard pressed. "Just tell me why you are taking us along?"

"Keep walking," Cavallo ordered. "I don't have to answer you nothing." Then, as if he finally heard the question, "Because this way they won't know who is breaking out. Get it?"

Brocard immediately saw the flaw. Cavallo had the gun; Cavallo, the plumber, knew the intricate maze of tunnels; and Cavallo had taken both Andy and him hostage. Who, in all likelihood, would the lieutenant in Center Control finger as the leader of the escape?

Andy also saw the stupidity of Cavallo's logic. But rather than point out the obvious, he angled to learn one more thing before Cavallo ran off into the Pennsylvanian fields.

"You know they are waiting to pick me up," Andy said. "That's what was planned. What are they going to say when you appear? Tell me that."

"They're going to say, 'Hello, Cavallo, here we are.' No one ever wanted you. What can you do for the don, anyway? All those E-mails weren't for you. They were for me."

Andy thought back over the schemes of the last few months. The chaos in the prison would mask his escape. Andy, sure, he would bring Cavallo with him. Everyone could do with a good lay, and Cavallo was the best. He was like a puppy to Andy: a puppy with a big cock. Nothing more. It boggled Andy's mind to imagine that it was Cavallo that Castellano wanted all along.

By now Brocard's back was aching: too many pipes and too much bending for someone who was woefully out of shape. Andy was also beginning to tire, not physically so much as psychologically. There was too much information for him to sort out. Yet there were some things he still needed to know.

"How did you get to know Don Castellano?" he asked, his voice shaking with rage. "E-mail him, did you? Send him a photo of your ass?" Brocard worried that Andy's invidious questions might set off Cavallo. He, unlike Andy, had not forgotten that the erstwhile plumber held a loaded gun. But Brocard underestimated Cavallo's tolerance for tactless questions, especially ones spiced with dirty references. He was a creature of the jails, after all, and used to being "pushed up on."

"Turn right and sit down over there, the two of you. Back to back." Cavallo put down the gun to retrieve from his pocket the cord he had brought to tie them up with. Brocard and Andy both saw the gun sitting on the ground a few feet away, but neither moved to snatch it up. Brocard felt tired and slow, and anyway, it simply wasn't his style. Andy knew he was a thief abandoned by thieves, a living, breathing cliché, and having nowhere to go, he wanted some answers at least.

As devastating as the whole affair had been, Andy was unable to conceal a frisson of excitement as Cavallo tightened the cord around his waist and pulled back his arms so tightly that he was absolutely powerless. As was often the case, Brocard could not for the life of him figure out what was going on.

"You're not the only one who likes to get their lips around it," Cavallo sneered.

"You're not trying to tell me you know Castellano," Andy replied incredulously.

"When I was out on parole, back in '94, then again in '98 and 2000—sure, I knew him, and he knows what I got and how I can use it."

"Liar. You've never sold your ass in Italy. You've barely made it to Jersey."

"Didn't have to. The Don comes to Philly, you see. But I'm going over there. He wants me over there now. 'Cause I do what he wants, when he wants it. And he likes that."

Though Cavallo took his time with the cord, he proved unskilled at tying knots; in fact, they were able to escape of their bonds within minutes of his departure. Cavallo had scooted up the staircase and out into the fields—which were completely unguarded because the Chief had so foolishly chosen to tighten the perimeter. He had made his way to a waiting car and begun to change his clothes as Brocard and Andy, exhausted from their ordeal but relieved to be free, climbed out into the night air. Relaxing in the car and anticipating the flight to Zurich, Cavallo began to play with his cock. His driver smiled, beholding the reason for his passenger's royal treatment. And, as Cavallo shot high and long into the night air, both of them laughed, knowing that the Don, who enjoyed watching his men get off like this, would want them to be pleased. "Feels good to be free, man," was all Cavallo said. Then, confident of his invulnerability, he drifted off to sleep.

The night air held no peace for either Brocard or his clerk. In the distance they watched as great plumes of smoke rose from Brotherly Love and heard the sirens of fire engines and emergency medical vehicles. The worst had indeed happened. Cheap wiring, poorly designed air ducts, and highly flammable insulation produced a fire that threatened to engulf the entire institution. With Internal Affairs working independently of FEET, who were walking away from the isolated warden, that was exactly what happened.

As they sat in the damp grass, Brocard and Andy expected a helicopter to descend and pick them up or, at the very least, for a surveillance truck to shine lights on them and tell them to freeze. But nothing of the kind happened. Instead, they lay in the field, waiting for nothing in particular, puzzled by all that had happened.

"You really did use me and your situation in the chapel, Andy," Brocard said glumly.

"Father, I'm a criminal," the clerk stated flatly. "A career one at that. That's the way it is. Besides, as you know, my pay scale was $2 a day. *A day,* Father. Didn't your mother ever tell you, you get what you pay for? All things considered, I think you got off pretty damn good."

"Tell, me, Andy, since everything is out in the open now anyway, just how big was this operation. Just how much was going on?"

"More than you, more than anyone could imagine," he replied haughtily. Then, pausing to consider what he had said, he added, "maybe even more than I imagined." In no rush to leave the limited freedom of the lawn, he closed his eyes and breathed in the acrid smoke as he collected his thoughts.

"It wasn't just that there were drugs and liquor in the jail," he continued. "There's nothing very big about that. No, this place was a depot, a distribution center, if you will, for central Pennsylvania. Straight up to the Catskills in New York, from what we heard. It was a perfect front, when you think about it. Trucks could come and go without ever being stopped by the local police. Prison World has its own cops, and they are all so underpaid, they just bought into things. There's truckloads of contraband out by the trailers." At this he waved his hand magisterially towards the far end of the field. "And I wouldn't be surprised if after all this goes down, after they put out the fires and lock up the inmates, those trucks don't just start right up and make their deliveries. It's mob stuff, bigger than all these jokers here. Everyone knows it, and no one is going to do anything about it."

Brocard found something rather refreshing about the fact that it was not only he who had been "played out," as the inmates would put it, but the jail and the entire region as well. But while Brocard had to admit he admired Andy's honesty, he was far too Catholic to accept such a pessimistic assessment of human nature.

Having worked out this much of the puzzle, Brocard suddenly felt very old and very tired. As for the *Palermo Caravaggio*, he was happy to leave that to Zinka and her injections of youth-giving hormones.

Forty

IMAGINE, IF YOU WILL, A GREAT SYMPHONIC work in which two entirely different modes, one minor and the other major, and two completely opposite tempi, one largo and the other presto, are played at the same time. Throughout most of the piece they each go their discordant way, seemingly oblivious one to the other. Then suddenly, at the very end, they unite to achieve a perverse harmony unlike anything anyone could have imagined. This is how the final chapter of the recovery of the *Palermo Caravaggio* played out. And only when this strange music is heard does its logic begin to make sense.

After spending years sequestered in a vault and enduring the brutal hands of thieves and the indelicate instruments required for its restoration, the great painting finally was to see light again. Its surface would feel the breeze of a summer's day and the image of the Holy Family captured on its surface would be admired again.

To accomplish such a transfer, Castellano had hand-picked the movers. These were no ordinary thugs, but a pair of well-heeled, downright elegant criminals, both of whom could be trusted to hold their tongues and wash their hands. They took their charge seriously, knowing that if any ill befell the painting, they would know no mercy. Castellano had his priorities and, good Italian that he was, the patrimony of Italy, especially when it was his alone, topped the list.

With painstaking deliberation, the workers covered the painting in bubble-wrap, carefully placed it in Porthault sheets, then removed it from the vault on the Bahnhofstrasse to set it on its journey to the villa on the far side of the lake. No cortege ever moved with such gravity. No head of state was ever afforded such solemnity.

This then was the major key, played largo. The basso continuo for the frantic activity, the presto of the symphony, was provided by Professoressa Zinka Pavlic, who kept things, and everyone, hopping at the villa.

"A wig, do you hear me?" she cried desperately. "There has to be one somewhere. Just get it." Zinka knew that if her ruse were to work, she had to disguise herself so that Cavallo, who she hoped had arrived by now, would not recognize her. But were some subtle lighting, some artfully arranged furniture, and artificial hair going to be enough to effect disguise?

Camille ran from the room, having no clue where to find one. She had seen her Zinka in moods like this before and knew full well that logic was irrelevant. Action, however misguided and unproductive, was the only proper response to her anxiety. Click your heels and flap your arms about and, in time, Zinka would snap out of it.

"Now you," Zinka said to Henry, who was planting a listening device in a vase of flowers, "hurry with that and help me move these bloody chairs about."

From the hallway outside the room where Zinka was spinning out of control, Camille heard her rough-handling the furniture. Something crashed against the wall. And, as luck would have it, she caught the rustling of starched aprons—that siren call of the scantily clad maids scattered about the place purely for visual effect.

"Mademoiselle," Camille said haltingly. She was not good at these things. "May I have a word?" Soon the young thing stood at her beck, tits pushed out and a smile frozen on her eager face. Now, just how do you ask someone if the hair they are sporting is in fact their own? Still, for Zinka's sake, she knew she had to ask. After she managed to pose the question, she was delighted to let the maid take her by the hand and escort her to a closet where props for every form of feminine deception were stored.

"There, no, over there, and a bit more to the right," Zinka commanded Henry. "Now close the curtain and turn on the light on the end table." Inspector Henry was starting to lose patience with Zinka and her ordering him about like some common servant. But he had quickly learned to give way when Zinka was on a tear. "The light has to come from one direction and cast a shadow, don't you see?"

Meanwhile, the painting had made its noble way down to the pier at the foot of the Bahnhofstrasse. Its chaperones ever so carefully placed it in Castellano's treasured 1950 Chris-Craft. The vessel, a glorious example of American motor boats, was unique to Lake Zurich: sleek timbers of polished mahogany off-set by shining brass fixtures. There the painting began her measured journey past villas and villages, docks and chapels, to her final destination. As she did, her two movers—not unlike Shakespeare's gravediggers—considered the absurdity of what they were doing.

"He's *pazzo*, man. Crazy I tell you."

"You're crazy if you don't lower your voice. Get back here nearer to the engine so it'll drown us out." Removing themselves to the back of the boat so that the pilot couldn't overhear them, and lighting up a couple of those nasty little cigarettes with no filters, they continued.

"This painting, I hear it's worth millions. And it's hot. What the hell is he doing parading this thing around? Why is he taking this risk, man? I mean, it's crazy."

"We both know why. The animal with the tits. She's eating him alive and he loves it." They both chuckled at the thought. They had worked for Castellano for years and knew his tastes. This woman, whoever she was, was it. On top of it, she had brains.

"I heard she knows about paintings, and this thing is one of the best. Caravaggio, you know. The Renaissance guy—did all the pope's rooms and everything."

"That was Michelangelo, you asshole." Then, taking a long puff, the thug with the answers explained that this was a baroque painting. "Yeah, baroque, don't you know?"

"And what exactly is that, asshole?"

"Just smoke your cigarette and shut up, will you?"

Despite the tranquil pace of their journey past the houses of the wealthy, there was too much to say to keep quiet.

"It's sex, you know."

"What's sex?" the dimmer of the two wondered. Then, reconsidering he added, "Sure, it's sex. What else?"

"He can't get it and has to have it so he'll do anything to be near it."

Strange as this arrangement might be to outsiders, it made perfect sense to anyone who was part of Castellano's inner circle. You could lose your life if you talked to anyone except those whom he needed to aid him in his obsession. These two were clearly among the elect.

"So do you recognize the pretty boy up in the cockpit with the pilot?"

"Sort of looks familiar. All I know for sure is that we have to deliver him with the painting. A package deal was the orders."

"That's the American from Philly with the massive cock that won't quit. Seems things were getting too hot for him in some jail, so the don had him sprung. Wants to have him perform again, I figure."

"More risks. Bringing big-prick over here—what, to see the masterpiece?"

"Which one?" They had a good laugh. But it was short-lived.

"It's a risk. A stupid risk the old man is taking."

"Probably makes it sexier for him. You know, the danger thing. Doing it on a balcony where everyone can see."

"Shit. He plans to do that, does he?"

"No, asshole. That's just like a delusion or whatever they call it. Poetic-like."

Silence reigned for a while as they tried to figure out their situation. Then, as the engines were cut and the motorboat began to dock, they said the same thing at the same time.

"Zurich." One started the next sentence, "Nobody is going to bother anybody," and the other finished, "in fucking Zurich." They were mistaken, of course. Times do change, and there are fewer and fewer places to hide. Especially for the foolish rich.

Zinka intended one final touch that simply had to be in place before the fateful encounter. She needed a bell, a tiny bell with which to signal a servant (or to call for help, should her plans go awry). Camille, God bless her soul, had seen one and went to fetch it as Zinka removed her panties and lubricated her ass. Once again she lamented that thousands of dollars had not bought her the vagina for which she had longed for. Fortunately, her colossal, well trained ass more than compensated for that shortcoming.

"Fine," Zinka bellowed when Camille returned. "Now put the bell on the library table—not there, you idiot, on the little table for books behind the chaise longue—and leave me." Now that the room had been staged like some gigantic Caravaggio-esque painting, with deep runnels of light and great pools of darkness, neither Camille nor Inspector Henry wanted to leave. "Get out I say!"

Her heart raced as Zinka stood alone in the great study where Castellano had told her to await the arrival of the *Caravaggio* and "a surprise." By now, she had guessed her surprise had recently escaped from Brotherly Love Pen. Were it he, she hoped the combination of her disguise, the dramatic lighting, and his jet lag would conspire to hide her identity. Even if it wasn't the Horse, she knew the real reason Castellano brought the *Palermo Caravaggio* out of hiding had nothing to do with its authentication or restoration. It had to do with risk and sex.

She also knew why he had chosen the room: They had used

it once before. He liked to see her ravished, worshiped, and abused. He would have done the job himself, had his penis been up to it, so to speak. In fact, he placed beautiful people and sex in the same category as fine cars and motor boats. If you could afford to, why not get someone else to take care of them and drive them for you. Why not simply lie back, feel the upholstery, and enjoy the ride.

The door opened, and the two overdressed brutes who had escorted the painting to the villa carried it dramatically to the large easel covered in velvet that Zinka had prepared for its arrival. Her throbbing heart sang when she caught sight of the liberated masterpiece. As restraint was not in her emotional vocabulary, she ran over to it as if it were a long-lost lover and stood transfixed but hardly silent. "My God, it is more beautiful than I had imagined—the chiaroscuro!" she exclaimed.

But Castellano had still more treasures for her as he slid into the room to witness the show of shows. Zinka turned to see Cavallo—shirt open, trousers off, and cock at the ready—waiting to perform his act. Suddenly, any fears she might have had vanished. He was the same dumb stud she had known in jail, so self-involved and cock-centered, she imagined he wouldn't even see her. *Maybe that's how he keeps it up,* she thought. Having been a man once, she remembered how they tended to turn people into objects to get off. From the way he was handling his cock—which, she had to admit was extremely impressive—she knew he could think of little else except where to plant it. She had at least one idea. But before they commenced, there were some things Zinka hoped to capture on tape. She knew she would have no problem getting what she needed, as the men surrounding her were saturated with testosterone and incapable of self-control.

"Nothing," she said to Castellano, "makes me hornier than masterpieces."

"*Carissima Professoressa,* write about them, study them, stand naked in front of them. There are more to excite you."

"You mean," she said, squealing like a pig to please him, "we can get more out of that nasty little hole of a vault to study and to get turned on by? Oh, Pappy!"

"For you, my goddess," he said, leading her over to Cavallo and unfastening the clip on the back of her dress, which dropped gracefully to the floor, "I will give anything, so long as you, too, give."

Zinka tried to keep well in the shadows to conceal her identity. Thanks to the massive wig Camille had procured for her—and to Cavallo's preoccupation with his massive tool—preserving her anonymity posed no problem.

"And you, stud," her voice was limpid as she spoke to Cavallo, "You're Pappy's cock, are you?" Cavallo groaned his assent. "What else would you do for Pappy? Would you rob for him, would you?" She pressed her body against his. "Would you kill for Pappy? Would you?" For this question, Zinka needed more than a grunt, so she took his cock in her hand and pulled violently. "Yes!" Cavallo shouted out, "yes!"

At this point the two rhythms and two modes of the symphony blended into a strange and haunting harmony. Zinka's frenzy vanished as she allowed her breasts to be worshiped. And the Holy Family of the *Palermo Caravaggio,* blushing slightly at such a display, positively glowed with anticipation as its moment of redemption neared. She emitted the occasional groan, not deeply felt but expected at such moments. Zinka raised her ass to sit on Cavallo face-to-face, then slid up and down, up and down, until his pulse raced and the moment neared.

"Come here and watch, old man." Zinka beckoned huskily. It was a summons Castellano could not refuse. "Watch it go in and know that it is you doing it. It's like your cock."

Castellano's back was so bad that he had never before considered bending over to closely observe a man penetrating a woman; however, the thought was simply too exciting to refuse. But the moment he did, Zinka pressed down so hard that Castellano's head was pinned under Cavallo's butt. Cavallo, in turn, was seized in Zinka's enormous storm-trooper right arm. The force of her move dislodged her wig and Cavallo instantly recognized Zinka, the behavior mod teacher. Sadly for him, it was too late to do anything about the revelation.

With her free hand, Zinka rang the bell on the library table to signal the end. Inspector Henry rushed in, followed by several officers who'd been staking out the villa, and Camille, the long-suffering girlfriend. She was proud of her Zinka, even though the methods she used to resolve the case were so frighteningly unconventional.

"Inspector," Zinka Pavlik, the cunning sleuth, said triumphantly, "I have your men!"

Epilogue

SHE WAS LATE. BUT THEIR APPOINTMENT could wait. After the painting had spent 400 years in an out-of-the-way oratory and several years in an airless vault, Brocard could wait a few more hours to set his gaze on the *Palermo Caravaggio*.

And as he was to meet his old friend Zinka, notoriously late for everything, on a summer's day in Naples, a time and place removed from schedules, the very issue of punctuality was absurd. Still, as he stood at the curb outside the grand old pile of a monastery where he lodged, he regretted he hadn't chosen a more comfortable place to rendezvous. One with chairs, and a bottle of mineral water, say. However, always one to make the best of any situation, no matter how bleak, Brocard leaned back against the crumbling wall, careful not to get too much plaster on his new clerical suit, and took out a copy of Avertanus's recent E-mail to study one last time.

My dearest Brother Brocard,

How relieved I am to hear that justice has prevailed, that the culprits who brought chaos to your jail
have been identified, and that your much sought-after
treasure, the beautiful painting of the Holy Family, is
finally safe. A caution, dear brother, as well. Although
you now see a series of dastardly schemes—although
you now think of creatures like your clerk and even that
oversexed Mafia tool as hapless creatures caught up in
a web of evil—I still see the hand of the evil one. How
relieved I am to know that you are out of that place and
away from those people. The devil is beguiling, my dear
friend. Make no mistake about it. He nearly caught you
this time, I believe, but as you live under the mantel of
Our Lady as a Brother of Divine Succor, she surely protected you more than you can even imagine. You remain
in my prayers, as I know I do in yours.

—Avertanus

Brocard was not sure how to answer his old friend. The jail
was rubble, but he had not yet resigned. Part of him still felt
compelled to continue prison ministry, futile as it might often be.

Officer Thomas never recovered from the trauma of being
trussed like a turkey. He suffered such a severe nervous break-
down that he was unlikely ever to see the inside of a jail, or a
church for that matter, again.

Most of the inmates were transferred to other prisons with
little or no time added to their sentences. Andy, in fact, was looking at a parole date. It would not have shocked Brocard, whose
tolerance for rough life had grown exponentially behind bars, to
learn Andy had worked out a deal with Jonathan to pimp the boy
on the street. Nothing base, mind you. They had in mind a
designer Web-site escort service in which both of them saw a
bright future.

Bear was sent to the new state gang prison just outside Harrisburg. This jail promised to be an economic boon to the local economy—and to the *ñeta* as well. They never missed a business opportunity, and had already managed to make the best of the situation. Unfortunately, Jesucito ended up in a ward for the criminally insane, where his self-mutilation might be observed and perhaps even treated. Cuchifrito also landed at the gang jail, where he would continue to meet the musical needs of his fellow felons.

Happily, Warden Boggs not only kept her job but also received a commendation for her levelheadedness in a difficult situation. This was pure bunk, but as Prison World was over-insured and made out handsomely on this whole affair, the company had no complaints about the warden's conduct. In fact, they now had the opportunity to build a maximum security, fully computerized and automated facility, without educational programs or remedial services: exactly what they and the surrounding community wanted.

This did not sit well with Tamara Boggs, who, for all her failings, at least had a heart. In discussing this matter with her new friend Kris Pouri, she found they shared a common vision: to speak out against prison injustice. During these late-night talks they decided to strike out on their own. They eventually established a nonprofit agency to advise communities, prisons, and anyone else willing to pay for their help.

Of course, Kris knew full well that Tamara had more in mind: something of a sexual, if not a domestic nature. Straight though she was, Kris was simply tired of expending energy on cross-gender relationships. For the time being, at least, a little quality time with a sister wouldn't hurt her at all.

Just then a horn blew. Out of the swirling Neapolitan traffic, as dramatic as Venus on a half shell, the glorious Zinka pulled up in a limousine far too wide for Southern Italy. She had on Pavarotti's earliest recording of Donizetti's *L'Elisir d'Amore,* her favorite opera by her very favorite composer. The music provided the perfect atmosphere for their jaunt up to the top of the mountain—the Capodimonte—where *their* painting (for now they considered it truly theirs) was temporarily housed.

They couldn't stop talking. Well, actually, Zinka couldn't. There were times when Brocard held his own; Zinka always required astute questions to keep her on target.

"Yes," she said breezily, "they had enough evidence to force the Swiss authorities to unseal the vault. What they found is absolutely amazing. Another vault held modern paintings. A load of crap, mostly, but big names. It will make for a fabulous article in *Flash Art*." Before she came up for air, she mentioned she would write yet another, far more scholarly article for *Burlington* about the restoration of their painting.

Brocard, of course, was more interested in discussing prison reform. The siege at Brotherly Love sparked a national debate about the safety of privately run prisons and the sanity of unsupervised programming. Fortunately, only a few heartless voices proposed to abandon programs completely. Brocard believed all had not been in vain.

How peaceful they felt as they gazed at the great Caravaggio's *Holy Family,* with the bizarre angel swooping down. Content as they were with a job well done, Brocard and Zinka couldn't help wondering what mischief they might get up to next.